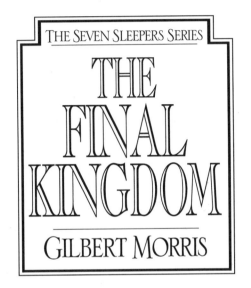

THE SEVEN SLEEPERS SERIES

THE FINAL KINGDOM

GILBERT MORRIS

MOODY PRESS
CHICAGO

Moody Press, a ministry of the Moody Bible Institute,
is designed for education, evangelization, and edification.
If we may assist you in knowing more about Christ
and the Christian life, please write us without obligation:
Moody Press, c/o MLM, Chicago, Illinois 60610.

©1997 by
GILBERT MORRIS

ISBN: 0-8024-3693-5

5 7 9 10 8 6 4

Printed in the United States of America

To Chris Meeks
I wish every young man in the country
were as dedicated as you, Chris.
May you be blessed every step of your way.

Contents

1
Final Call to Battle

A sullen, hot sun beat down upon the weary travelers winding their way along the mountainous road. Their feet raised tiny puffs of dust that rose in the almost motionless air, then fell back to earth.

The last member of the procession—a smallish fifteen year old with red hair—stopped abruptly and pulled off his hat. He yanked a handkerchief from his pocket, wiped the grime from his face, spat on the ground, and called out, "I'm tired of eatin' all this dust! Let *me* go in front for a while."

The leader of the hikers, tall, gangling Josh Adams, did not even break stride. Auburn hair peeped out from under the wide-brimmed straw hat he had on. He kept his light blue eyes fixed on the road ahead as he called back sharply, "Stop complaining, Jake! We've all had to take our turn in the back."

Jake Garfield jammed his hat onto his head and plunged forward, sending up choking clouds of dust. "I don't see why we can't wait until it rains. This dust is killing me—I can hardly breathe!" He looked off to the low-lying mountains on one side and abruptly ran into the youth in front of him. "Why don't you pick up your feet, Wash!" Jake snapped, giving the boy a shove.

Wash, who had been born with the rather grand title of Gregory Randolph Washington Jones, caught his balance. The heavy knapsack on his back pulled him backwards, and he grunted involuntarily. The smallest boy of the party, Wash had ebony black skin and large, innocent brown eyes. Now he rolled those eyes wildly.

"Watch where you're going, Jake! Them big clodhoppers of yours are enough to sink a battleship!" Wash was good-natured, however, and turned around to wink at Jake. "If you ever grow into your feet, you'll be a big fellow, sure enough."

Sarah Collingwood, marching along behind Josh, was small and graceful with brown eyes and black hair. Dust coated her hair just now, and her face was tense from their long march. She hooked her thumbs under the straps of her knapsack. Pulling at them to ease the discomfort, she groaned. "I'm so thirsty I'm spitting cotton. Can't we stop and find a stream somewhere?"

"Me, too, Sarah—I'm ready to drop." The speaker just behind Sarah was Abbey Roberts, a pretty blue-eyed blonde, who was at the moment extremely irritable. "This dust is under my fingernails, in my hair, up my nose. I'll *never* get clean again! We've got to stop!"

Josh gave a heavy sigh. "All right, have it your own way—but we'll never get to Dothan at this rate."

"Hey—look over there—I think I see a line of trees. Maybe there's a creek alongside them." Reb Jackson was tall, lean, muscular. Traces of the old South were in his speech, and the journey had not worn him down as much as it had the others. He was tough as a piece of leather, and now he shoved his sweaty tan Stetson back on his head and squinted against the bright sun. "I'll go see how she looks. You come when I holler." He left the line of march, broke into a half run, and soon was hidden in a gully.

"I wish I was as tough as that fellow," Dave Cooper said. At seventeen, he was the oldest of the Seven Sleepers. He was tall and athletic, though the weary trek had worn him thin at the moment. He wore a white cotton shirt, yellowed now with the thick dust of the road, and he took off a light felt hat to wipe his brow. He continued walking, his blue eyes searching the gully for Reb. "There he is—waving his hat. I expect he's found water."

"Well, let's go," Josh said wearily. "But we'll have to make better time tomorrow to make up for today."

"I don't see how we can do any better tomorrow," Jake mumbled as they left the road and trudged through thin grass toward where Reb stood at the line of trees. "We've been practically running all day."

"I guess Josh is afraid we'll be late," Wash said. "After all, somebody's got to keep this bunch on the move."

"We've been on the move for weeks," Jake stated flatly. "We won't be any good when we do get there at this rate. We'll be so dried out we won't be able to even *hear* Goél—much less do what he says!"

Wash shrugged and said nothing. He was accustomed to Jake's grumbling. Now, however, he felt there was some ground for it—the Sleepers had been hard driven.

As he plodded along, Wash thought of the strange life into which he had fallen. He had been born in the slums of a great city. If nothing had happened to redirect him, he would have probably joined a gang and perhaps been shot in one of the drug wars that raged there incessantly.

But he had not met that fate. Along with the other six Sleepers, he had been chosen and placed in a sleep capsule just before nuclear war swept the earth. Time passed, and Wash lay in his capsule oblivious to the raging fires, explosions, and terrible changes that took place on earth. Finally the Sleepers had been awakened and came forth to find the world that they had known gone forever. They were now inhabitants of Nuworld, where mutations had created strange beings such as giants, snakepeople, and dragons.

Wash kept his eye on the figure of Reb, waiting ahead, and thought of the adventures they had experienced together under the leadership of Goél. At first Wash had not understood Goél, but now he knew that their strange leader was the only hope of Nuworld. The Sleepers had immediately discovered that Nuworld was under the dominion of a sinister being called the Dark Lord. It was only the force of Goél that kept the Dark Lord from tyrannizing and enslaving the entire planet.

Wash thought of how they had fought Goél's battles, narrowly escaping death many times, and wondered what task lay ahead for them. They had been summoned to a council, where the leaders of the House of Goél would rendezvous on the Plains of Dothan.

The Sleepers had been halfway across the globe when the summons came. Their trip had already involved scaling high mountains, sailing treacherous waters, fighting hunger and thirst across desert plains —but now, hopefully, they would soon be at the gathering.

Josh slipped his knapsack from his shoulders and stretched painfully. He did not want to show weakness, but he felt drained and knew that he could not have gone on much farther himself. Looking down at the small stream that wound in snakelike fashion through the rocks, he said, "Well, let's make camp here. We'll eat and get a good night's sleep."

Sarah began going through her pack and shook her head. "We don't have much food left. I'll do the best I can."

"I'll make a fire," Reb said. "Wash, do you and Dave want to help me drag up some of that firewood?" Tired as they were, they all eagerly joined in the business of setting up camp. They had become experts at this, for they had camped out under many strange skies and in dangerous places. Soon the tent that the girls shared was up, the blankets for the boys rolled out, and the smell of cooking meat on the air.

By the time the food was ready, the red sun was sinking rapidly into the horizon. The boys plopped down, eager for the meal that Sarah and Abbey were preparing.

"I'm hungry enough to eat a skunk!" Reb declared. He was sitting cross-legged. His eyes were bright as Sarah passed him a chunk of meat roasted over the open fire.

"This isn't skunk," she said, "but it's all we have."

"Actually what is it, Sarah?" Dave asked.

"It's part of that last antelope that Reb shot three days ago."

"Huh!" Jake grunted as he took his share. "Must be gettin' a little ripe by now. It'll probably make us all sick." Nevertheless, he chewed with evident enjoyment.

Sarah divided the meat as evenly as she could and then said, "We've only got six potatoes. How do you divide six into seven?"

"Just give me Wash's potato." Reb grinned. "He doesn't like potatoes anyhow."

"You keep your mouth off my potato," Wash protested. "I wish it was a sweet potato, though."

They wrangled for a while. Finally Dave settled the problem by sharing his potato with Abbey. "I'm the only mathematician around here," he said. He put some of the steaming potato into his mouth, then joggled it around fiercely. "Wow, that's hot!"

11

"Baked potatoes always are." Abbey smiled. "Don't be so greedy."

The Sleepers made the meal last as long as they could. When they came back from enjoying drafts of fresh water from the brook, Sarah said, "I've got a surprise. I saved these for a special treat." She pulled four apples out of her bag and smiled. "Dessert. I kept them, but how do you divide four into seven? That's worse than six potatoes and seven people."

"Just let me have Reb's and Dave's." Wash laughed. "That way I think it'll come out even."

Sarah managed to distribute close to equal slices.

Josh took his portion and said, "You're a miracle, Sarah! You keep dredging up food when you think we're all out." He bit into the apple and chewed thoughtfully. "It's almost as sweet as those that grew in the orchard out behind our house back in Oldworld."

"I remember those," Sarah said dreamily. "But I don't think these are near as good."

Josh and Sarah had been close friends in Oldworld, and he thought that now they were closer than ever. They had been little more than children when they had been snatched out of their homes and placed in the sleep capsules, but now they were quickly approaching maturity. They sat apart from the others, for a time saying little. Finally, Josh demolished all of his apple except for a fragment of core. He stared at it thoughtfully. "I'd like to have four or five of those."

"You'd have a stomachache if you did. Remember how you ate those green apples back when you were fourteen? I thought we'd have to take you to the hospital. I never heard such hollering and carrying on." Sarah's brown eyes held a trace of fond amusement.

Eventually fatigue drove the Sleepers to bed. To Josh's dismay, they slept late the next morning, and the sun was high in the sky when they finally dragged themselves out of their blankets.

Reb looked at the creek and said, "I'm gonna fish a little bit. We gotta have something fresh to eat."

Josh was already shaping his blanket into a roll. "We don't have time for that. Better get ready."

"I reckon we've got time to catch a fish," Reb argued.

"You heard what I said, Reb! Get your bedroll pulled together. We've got to get out of here."

Reb stared at him, his face reddening. "The rest of you go on, Josh. I'll catch some fish and catch up with you."

"We can't be separated," Josh snapped. "I don't want to argue about it anymore."

"I'm not arguing," Reb stated. "I'm just going to do what I said."

Sarah laid a hand on Reb's arm. "I'd like to have some fresh fish too, Reb, but we're running late. And we don't want to miss the gathering, do we?"

Josh could see that the Southerner was angry, but Sarah's soft words seemed to draw most of the anger from him.

Reb said shortly, "Well, all right then—but I think it's plumb foolish."

Ten minutes later they had broken camp and were on the road again. A light drizzle began and settled the dust. The ground underfoot became somewhat muddy, but Josh was relieved not to be breathing yellow powder.

When they stopped for a midmorning break, he went to sit by himself under a spreading tree at the roadside.

Sarah came over and sat beside him. "Don't be angry at Reb. He's just wound up tight—like all of us."

"I know it," Josh said immediately. He was a gentle-spirited boy, not at all certain of his abilities. He often felt that someone else—someone such as Reb, who was the best fighter—should be the leader of the Sleepers. Goél had named Josh, however, and he had to obey.

Picking up a stick, he drew a meaningless figure in the dirt. Silence had fallen over the land, and a slight breeze had risen. Looking up, Josh said wearily, "We can't go on much longer, Sarah." There was a touch of defeat in his voice. "I don't like to talk like that, but it looks to me like the Dark Lord is winning. We're getting pinned down all over the world. Everywhere we go, the Sanhedrin has its spies."

"But think of how many we've helped, Josh. If we hadn't gone to the land of the Amazons, for example, the Dark Lord would have won the whole tribe over."

"Oh, sure." Josh shrugged his lean shoulders. "We're winning a little—but the Dark Lord's servants are everywhere. They're like . . . like a cloud of locusts. And you can't kill them by stepping on them one at a time."

Sarah said quietly, "I think everything's coming to a focal point."

"What does that mean?"

"I mean—well, there's something *important* about this summons to come to the Plains of Dothan. I think that we're going to find out something exciting from Goél."

Josh nodded slowly. "He did say something the last time about a final battle." He took a deep breath and tried to smile. "I hope this is it. It's been a long, hard road the past couple of years."

Sarah put a hand on his arm. "You've done wonderfully well, Josh," she whispered. "No one could have led better than you."

14

Josh suddenly grinned and looked much younger than his sixteen years. "You always know how to make a fellow feel good, Sarah." He put his hand over hers and squeezed it. "But you're right. We'll make it. We might walk our legs off—but we'll make it."

The huge field called the Plains of Dothan lay at the base of some high-rising mountains to the east and the west. The Sleepers found the level floor of the plain swarming with activity.

Reb suddenly let out a yelp. "Look! There's Princess Elaine!" He ran ahead to greet a young woman mounted on a beautiful snow-white steed.

The girl wore a long white dress and a cone cap with a blue veil on the tip. She looked like a medieval princess, which was, in a way, what she was. Elaine came from the Nuworld land of Camelot, where people still lived the lives of knights and ladies and warriors.

Behind Elaine rode a troop of knights wearing armor that glistened like silver. They carried their lances high. Several laughed as Reb came to greet his old friend.

"My Reb!" Princess Elaine said. She came down from her horse and gave him her hands.

When Reb kissed them, a cry of laughter went up from the other Sleepers and from the knights.

Reb flushed but kept his head up. "How's my horse?"

"We're still keeping him for you. I've been expecting you to come back to Camelot every day since you left." The princess was looking up at Reb. "You have grown. You're a man now."

The other Sleepers, too, were meeting old friends from their past adventures. Jake ran at once to a tall man and a beautiful young woman who had large wings attached to their backs.

"Sureflight—and Loreen!" These were the winged warriors of the desert where Jake and the others had learned to fly. He approached them, grinning from ear to ear. "I was hoping you'd be here. Did you bring a set of wings for me?"

"No, you'll have to come back to our home," Loreen said.

She put out her hands, and Jake grabbed them and held them tightly. "It's so good to see you, Loreen!" he whispered. "I've been lonesome for you."

Sureflight looked down at his daughter and the young redhead, and amusement came to his eyes. "We have been waiting for you to come back. Loreen has been very lonely."

Jake looked quickly at Sureflight and then at the masses of people about them. "Looks like we've got a little business here first. I think there's some kind of trouble."

"You're right, Jake," Loreen said. "Goél's message for us said to bring all of our warriors as soon as we could. We came on ahead of them. There's going to be a battle—I think there's no doubt about that."

Josh and Sarah soon ran into Captain Ryland Daybright and the beautiful Dawn. Abbey and Dave and Wash saw still other old friends, and it was a pleasant time indeed. A meal had been prepared for the large company, and they ate and drank, enjoying a wonderful time of reunion.

And then a voice came over the air, clear and strong.

"Welcome, my friends, to the House of Goél!"

Instantly Josh knew that voice! He turned and saw a figure standing on a flat rock that rose above the floor of the plain. A tall man, wearing a light gray robe with the hood thrown back, he stood before the host, looking around him calmly.

Goél. The mysterious leader who carried the battle to the Dark Lord. He was burned by the sun, and his eyes were deep set and darkly brooding. His hands were corded with strength, and there was a powerful presence about him as he looked around at those who had come at his bidding.

"My faithful friends, you have come—and I thank you all. For years now you have fought the Dark Lord. Many of our comrades have fallen in the struggle—and some will fall in that one which is to come."

A voice called, "Is it time, Goél?"

"Yes! The time comes for the final battle. Will Nuworld be ruled by the tyranny of the Dark Lord, or will peoples everywhere come into the House of Goél and live as free beings should?"

The question seemed rhetorical, and he stood there for a time, apparently thinking. Then he began to tell them of many things, and no one moved as long as he spoke. At last, he said, "I will be giving you more instructions later—but for now, eat, and drink, and enjoy the fellowship of Goél."

Josh turned to Sarah. "Well, that tears it," he said. "We were right. There's going to be a final battle this time."

Sarah looked troubled. "It all sounds so—well, so *final*. What if we lose?"

Josh was silent. He did not want to consider that possibility.

The Sleepers continued to wander among the milling crowd, meeting more old friends. And then Goél himself appeared at Josh's side and greeted him warmly.

17

"And here is my faithful Joshua."

"Sire, we have come," Josh said. "But we have not the strength that we once had. I fear that we are worn thin."

Goél smiled at him. "You have done your best, and that is all that I ask of any of my servants. But the hour is near, and I must send you on a mission to alert three more groups of my people."

"Who are they, Goél?" Sarah asked, standing close beside Josh.

"You must go to the Land of Ice and to the Centaurs and to Celethorn, Land of the Magicians. It will be another long journey, but when those three groups are here, my host will be complete. I will not send you alone. I will have guides for you. Will you do this for me?"

Josh suddenly felt refreshed. The very presence of the tall man, and the warmth of his eyes, and the power that seemed to flow through him strengthened the boy. He said sturdily, "We will follow your orders as long as we draw breath, Goél!"

"That's my faithful Joshua!" Goél said warmly. "The Seven Sleepers are indeed my pride!"

2

Council of the Dark Lord

F ar to the north of the Plains of Dothan, where Goél
had summoned his subjects, a land fierce and terrible rose up out of the broken tableland. The trees of
that land were withered and stunted, as if compressed
by the air into bent, twisted shapes. Birds that would
sing merrily in brighter lands avoided the place. The
only sounds from the air above were the harsh croak-
ings of ravens as they crisscrossed the somber skies.

Travelers avoided this fearsome country, though
to do so meant detouring hundreds of miles through
difficult terrain—and those who were caught in it by
night sometimes did not live to regret it. When the
moon arose, strange beasts, foul and unnatural, issued
from caverns in the depths of this blasted land. It was
a deadly country, feared and despised by those inhabitants of Nuworld who had the misfortune to find themselves within its borders.

Winter gales swept across the bleak, hostile envi-
ronment, chilling to the bone and almost freezing the
teeth of unfortunate travelers. In the fall, the winds
pushed across the landscape as if seeking to shove
travelers off the narrow mountain paths into the val-
leys of broken rock far below. Spring and summer, a
time of joy and beauty in other parts of Nuworld,
brought forth only blistering sunshine that cooked the
rocks and baked the faces of those who hurried across
the region.

Far inland in the center of this terrible land, a circle of jagged mountains ringed a castle that rose out of the stones of the earth. The mountains, which served as a fortress wall against any who would attack, were broken by only three passes, kept guarded at all times by the servants of the Dark Lord. Woe be to those who attempted to pass through! Those who did come were more often brought as prisoners—and most were never seen again.

The castle itself was made of solid stone. No one knew how long it had stood there, but its rocks were blasted gray with age and crumbled with the fierce snows and blistering suns that had beaten upon them. Nor did anyone know *how* such a fortress was built. Those who studied it could only be puzzled, for it would have taken thousands of men thousands of years to build such a structure. Its turrets pierced the sky like daggers, and the rounded walls of those towers were slitted to allow bowmen to deal swift death to any who would attack. At times foul smoke would issue from the chimneys, choking those who had the misfortune to breathe it. Neither plant nor animal could endure its stench for long.

The Dread Tower rose like a skeletal finger in the center, and from its crest the entire land could be surveyed by the Dark Lord and his henchmen.

Inside that tower all was massive stone. Steps carved out of rock led down deep, deep, deep into the bowels of the earth, where dungeons kept their terrible secrets forever. Cries and muted screams rose from these chambers far beneath the Dread Tower. There was at least one huge room, known to none but the Dark Lord himself, where a massive brass gate was bolted to the solid rock, strong enough to secure any living thing. At times the Dark Lord would come and put his baleful eye on the huge gate.

The most cheerful spot in the Dread Tower was the council room. It was here the Dark Lord summoned his commanders from time to time to plot his strategy for overthrowing Goél and his House. Even now, that wicked crew sat around tables, tearing at food like vicious animals and swilling down dark, strong liquor. The Dark Lord did not join in these riotous festivities. He sat on a seat of stone, his clawlike hands clutching its arms. He was cloaked from head to foot in a black cape, his head hidden beneath a hood that fell over and concealed his countenance. Only the red gleam of his eyes could be seen by his captains as they glanced at him from time to time. Motionless, silent, fierce, the Dark Lord watched the revels of his dusky band.

Several vicious fights broke out as the rowdy feasting went on. Powerful, beastlike men pummeled each other. Once, swords were drawn, and their clash filled the council room. The Dark Lord made no effort to stop the duel, nor did the captains. All cried for their favorites, and when one lay on the floor, his eyes glazing in death, a cry of exultation went up from the supporters of his opponent, who raised his bloody sword high.

Finally the Dark Lord said, *"Hear me!"*

Instant silence fell across the chamber. The eye of every captain looked upward to where his lord sat on the dais, staring down at them. Not one, however, looked with love or admiration. Fear had brought them there, and fear kept them there. Every member of the horrid company knew that only strength would prevail with the Dark Lord. Failure was punished, sometimes with death—which was merciful—sometimes with something much worse.

The air seemed to grow heavy as each waited for the Dark Lord to speak.

At last he said, "The time has come."

The Dark Lord's voice echoed in the council room. Even the candles in their wall sockets seemed to bend with the force of it. "We have waited long enough! It is time to strike the final blow against the House of Goél!" His voice rose to a high pitch, filled with anger and frustration. "Goél must die and all who follow him!" The Dark Lord waited as shouts of agreement echoed, then he said, "I will hear what you have to offer as a method of ridding me of him."

Once again there was silence. All knew the penalty of rashness when dealing with this terrible being who sat watching them, his red eyes glowing. Few dared speak.

At last, however, a tall, thin form stood forth. This was Gnash, the victor in many of the Dark Lord's battles. His features were dark, and his teeth showed yellow as he grinned horribly. He wore a leather jerkin and a sword at his side, which he fingered constantly. "My lord," he said, "we are all aware of the problem of Goél and his accursed House."

A murmur of angry cries went up, and Gnash held up a hand to silence it.

"The answer, as we all know, is somehow bound up with the prophecy that came long ago." He hesitated, then quoted part of a prediction that had been circulated in Nuworld for many years: "'And when the Seven Sleepers wake—the House of Goél will be filled.'"

"You dare speak *that* in my presence?" The Dark Lord leaned forward and half lifted his hand, as if to send a lightning bolt and strike Gnash to the floor.

"Hear me, my dread lord," Gnash cried quickly,

blinking. "We cannot win by ignoring the problem. We must strike at the Seven Sleepers themselves."

His words seemed to appease the Dark Lord somewhat. He settled back in his chair, but there was a sneer in his voice as he said, "This is your answer, Gnash? Have you not tried, all of you, time and time again, to crush these accursed Sleepers? And all of you have failed! Seven babies—infants! And all the warriors of my kingdom cannot bring them to bay! *Faugh!* *You* are the infants and the babies!"

Gnash swallowed hard but managed to hold his ground. "We have failed—I admit it, my liege lord—but I have come to believe that there is more to these Sleepers than flesh and blood." He waved a hand. "Have we not trapped them again and again? Have we not thrown our forces against them when all hope for them was wiped out—and *still* they escaped?" Gnash shook his head grimly. "This is sorcery, my lord, and we must fight it. And no amount of swords or shields can overcome such protection as they apparently have."

Again, a murmur of agreement ran around the hall, and the flames in the fireplace leaped. The captains seemed hungry wolves as they leaned forward to hear what the Dark Lord would say.

"I think you may be right," he said grudgingly. "I have often thought this Goél—blast his name!—is not of this earth. He is no mere man, or he would have been crushed long ago. What is your remedy then, Gnash?"

"I believe we must take the Sleepers not through brute force but through craft and guile."

For some time the discussion went on. But though it was apparent that Gnash had spoken truth, no practical method of applying his remedy appeared.

The Dark Lord said crushingly, "Is this all of your help, my captains?"

"No, sire."

A heavy, bulky figure appeared to the Dark Lord's right. This was Morder, the chief of the council. There was a cruelty in the man that made even the brutal captains cringe as they watched him. His eyes were small and keen and had a yellowish tinge, peering out from under heavy brows. His skin was dark, and the hair of his head and beard was lank. Hair grew in tufts over his arms and neck as well. No one doubted his shrewdness.

"What is your word, Morder?" the Dark Lord asked. "You have never failed me. What now shall we do?"

"My lord," Morder said slowly, his voice as heavy and bulky as his form. "I have good news. We have placed an informer in the House of Goél."

"This has been tried before!" the Dark Lord said impatiently. "They have always ferreted out those we sent, no matter how clever."

"Indeed, you speak the truth, my lord—but this time I have succeeded. We now have an opportunity to know the inner secrets of the movements of Goél's people."

Gnash cried out at once, "If we have done that, then we can lay snares for them and they cannot escape! War is certain. We *must*—we *shall*—destroy the Sleepers!"

Every throat was suddenly filled with screams of anger and hatred for Goél.

The Dark Lord looked down upon the burly forms of his lieutenants. He lifted a hand and in the silence that followed said, "We must not fail. This Goél, despite all of our efforts, grows stronger. More and more of the free peoples of Nuworld are flocking to his banner. If we do not destroy him now, he will destroy us."

Morder said confidently, "Do not fear, my lord. We have the strength—and soon we shall have the knowledge—to trap the Seven Sleepers. Believe me, or let my head answer for it. I will have these Sleepers in the dungeons crying for death before long."

"Your head is pledge, then, Morder. See to it."

The Dark Lord leaned back and watched as the feast continued. He did not move, but his power seemed to fill the room.

Morder whispered to Gnash, "If we fail, you know the penalty."

Gnash said nervously, "This informer—is he a reliable spy?"

"Very reliable. No one would suspect. Do not fear —this time we will trap the Sleepers!"

25

3
Two Guides

The various elements of the army of Goél were busy. Ever since Goél had stated his intention of bringing on the final battle, men and animals and Nuworld creatures had constantly been brought into the camp. Weapons were sharpened and burnished, and supplies were laid in.

This place is like a gigantic beehive! Josh thought as he looked over the milling soldiers early one morning. He had risen early and breakfasted with the other Sleepers and now stood in the center of the plain, looking for Goél.

He found him in the midst of giving orders to several of his captains. Josh waited patiently, and finally he caught Goél's eye.

Smiling, Goél motioned Josh toward him. "Good morning, Joshua. Are your companions outfitted and ready?"

"Yes, sire," Josh said. "What is it you would have us to do?"

"Come with me, and I will give you your orders."

Josh walked alongside the tall form of his leader as they made their way through the teeming camp. Finally they found a fairly secluded spot in a grove of small trees. A little stream ran through the plain here, and Goél motioned to the bank. "Sit down, Joshua."

For a time they sat quietly, staring into the water that bubbled pleasantly over the stones. From far off came the faint sound of men practicing with their arms, but here it was still and peaceful.

"I wish every place was as quiet as this one," Josh said. He reached into the cool water and let it make a small wave over his palm. He caught some then and tasted it. "Good water," he said. "Cold and clear."

"You've had a difficult time, my son. I regret that I have used you so hard."

Josh looked up with some surprise. "That's what we were brought to Nuworld for, Goél. To serve you— to fill your House."

"Yes, but it is an expensive task," Goél said slowly. There was deep, almost bottomless, sadness in his eyes as he fixed them on Josh. "No kingdom is built without pain and sweat and blood. It is not easy to send good servants like you into deadly situations. You have been a joy to me, my Joshua."

The words warmed Josh's heart. As always, his weariness and fears fell away when he was in the presence of Goél. He smiled with pleasure. "We have done little," he said, shrugging. "Sometimes it seems so hopeless, Goél."

"I know. The Dark Lord has his armies—his terrible captains—roaming the earth. At times it seems that those of my House are being swallowed by the Dark Lord's dreadful strength."

"It does seem like that." Josh nodded. "If it wasn't for you, I would say it was impossible." He flushed and ducked his head. "As a matter of fact, I *have* said that a time or two."

"Never take counsel of your fears, Joshua," Goél said. Then he smiled. "You have come a long way from that callow boy who first came out of a sleep capsule. You have done battle in high places, and you have maintained your honor—and my honor, as well—in

28

times of stress and danger. No man could have done more."

Then Goél sighed heavily. "It *is* quiet here. I long for peace, even as you, my son. And that peace will come someday. Can you believe that?"

"I believe it if you say so, Goél."

"Good! But before the peace comes the war." He leaned toward Josh. "I think few recognize what a terrible battle this last one will be. We have not seen the Dark Lord's full strength put forth. His wicked servants have multiplied. They are scattered over the whole earth now, but he will draw them to this place soon. And here we must meet him. Every sword blade will count; every arrow and every club must count also. That is why I am now sending you and your company to bring in three groups that have not yet responded to my call."

"What are these three armies, sire?"

"I would not call them 'armies.' They are more like small tribes. But I repeat, it may be that one sword will make the difference as to which way the battle goes. We cannot spare one man, or one horse, or one blade."

"I understand, sire. Just give me the orders."

"You must go first to the Land of Ice, where you will speak to the chief of the Aluks. They are a hardy people, and they love me, but they know not of this battle. Give them the summons to come at once to the Plains of Dothan. Second, you must go to the Land of the Centaurs."

Josh lifted his head. "Centaurs?"

"You have heard of the centaurs?"

"Yes, but I didn't know they were real. You mean the half-horse and half-man people?"

"Exactly, and they are very powerful allies. Not just in their numbers, but they have powers that go beyond flesh and blood. You must convince them to come at once."

"And the third group?"

"The third group is more difficult."

"Are they your people, Goél?"

"Some of them are, but there is an element among them that fights against me. You must go to Celethorn, Land of the Magicians."

"Magicians?"

"You seem startled at that. Possibly 'magicians' is not the best word," Goél said quietly. "Wise men, perhaps. And wise women too. They have deep knowledge and powers, even beyond those of the centaurs. In the end it may be that the special powers they bring will be more important to the success of our battle than any sword of steel."

Josh repeated the orders. "We're to go to the Land of Ice, to the Centaurs, and to Celethorn, and to bid all to come to the Plains of Dothan."

"With all haste. It is vital."

"Do you have a map for us to follow?"

"I have something better than that. I have guides for you. Two of them. Tried and trusted in my service in the past. I will introduce you to them. Then you must be on your way."

Back in camp, Goél hailed a woman wearing a simple white garment with a belt of gold. It came barely to her knees, and her arms were free. On her back was a quiver, and she held in her hand a beautifully constructed bow.

"This is Glori. She will guide you to the centaurs and then to the Land of the Magicians. That is a difficult place to find, but she has been there before. Glori, this is Joshua Adams, the leader of the Seven Sleepers."

Glori was a woman of some thirty years, it appeared to Josh. She had striking light blue eyes and blonde hair, bound by a silver clip and hanging down her back. She smiled a greeting and said, "I had not expected one so famous to be so young."

Josh flushed and felt like kicking at a clod, so embarrassed was he at her praise. He could say nothing at all.

Goél spoke up. "Josh is a modest young man. He will need your help, Glori. Now, both of you come. You will also need a guide to the Land of Ice."

Josh and Glori followed him closely through the busy throngs to the outskirts of the camp, where some sturdy, swarthy dwarfs were thumping each other with clubs and wooden swords. They stopped their exercises and turned, puffing, to face Goél.

"Beorn!" he called.

One of the dwarfs approached at once. He was no more than four feet high but was as burly as a barrel. His arms and legs were thick with muscle, and his chest was deep. His glittering eyes were almost hidden behind the lank black hair that hung over his forehead.

"Yes, my lord." His voice was guttural, almost a grunt.

"This is Joshua Adams, who leads the Seven Sleepers. You will guide the Sleepers to the Land of Ice. No one knows the way better than you."

"It is a hard way," Beorn said, "and filled with danger, but I will guide them."

"Good. Afterward Glori will guide the Sleepers to the centaurs, then to Celethorn. You will accompany them. They will have need, perhaps, of your stout battle-ax."

"Do I take none of my companions?"

"No, you must travel lightly. Force will not avail.

You must be crafty, and I know you as the most crafty of all dwarfs."

Beorn looked at Josh, and his nostrils flared. "This one is weak," he said bluntly. "It will require a stronger than he to get through."

Josh flushed and almost snapped out an answer but managed to keep his lips tightly closed.

Glori, however, said, "You have not heard of the fame of the Seven Sleepers? They have overcome greater odds than this." Her tone was disdainful, and it was obvious that she did not care for the dwarf.

Goél smiled at Josh. "You will find Beorn a gifted guide and faithful to me. It would be useless to send more. You have done noble deeds in the past—now this one more time, my Joshua." He put his hands on Josh's shoulders. "I am putting great faith in you. You will not fail me."

"I will do my best, sire," Josh whispered.

When Goél had disappeared into the crowd, Josh turned to his two guides. "Let's go collect what you'll need to take along. We'll leave at once."

Beorn walked back to the other dwarfs, spoke rapidly to them, then picked up a heavy-looking knapsack and put it on his shoulder. It seemed to have no weight at all, so strong was he. In the other hand he carried a wicked-looking battle-ax with a razor-sharp edge.

Josh nodded approval, and the three left the dwarfs' practice field. They picked up Glori's gear, then Josh took them to the spot where the other Sleepers were waiting.

"This is Glori, who will be one of our guides. She will take us to two of our destinations, and this is Beorn, who will take us to our first task in the Land of Ice."

The Sleepers stared curiously at the strangers.

What a contrast! Sarah thought. *She's so beautiful, and he's so ugly!* Nevertheless, she stepped forward at once and offered her hand to Glori, saying, "We're grateful to have you." Then she turned to the dwarf, who was scowling at her. "And you are welcome too, my friend."

Beorn stared at her for a long moment, unsmiling. Sarah flushed. She took a step back as the rest greeted the two guides.

It was the same in each case. Glori greeted each Sleeper with a firm handshake and a kind word. The dwarf simply stood there, his hand on his battle-ax. Finally he said gutturally, "Do we stand here talking all day, or are we going to obey Goél?"

An hour later, the Sleepers and their guides were long out of sight of the camp. They were walking along, Josh still angry at the dwarf's rudeness, when the guttural voice spoke again. "And where do you think you're going?"

Josh swung around and saw that the dwarf had stopped and was staring at him with a sneer.

"What do you mean?" Josh asked.

Beorn waved a hand forward. "You'll never get to the Land of Ice that way," he said. "I thought *I* was to be the guide."

Josh flushed, and his freckles stood out. "All right," he said gruffly, "which way is it?"

Beorn did not answer. He strolled past Josh and made a right-angle turn without even looking to see if the others were following.

Sarah came up to Josh, who was glaring after the dwarf, and whispered, "Don't let him upset you, Josh.

He's grouchy—but after all, he *is* the one Goél gave us to show us the way."

Dave asked Glori, "Couldn't *you* show us the way?"

"I can take you to two of your destinations but not to the Land of Ice. That is Beorn's specialty. But he *is* a horrible sort of creature, isn't he?"

"He sure is." Jake drifted up to stand beside them. "I'm surprised that Goél uses him. He's not the kind you'd like to go on a two-week canoe trip with."

"Or any kind of trip with," Wash agreed. "But we better get after him. He looks like he's not going to slow down for us."

"All right," Josh said with grim determination, "let's show him the Sleepers can keep any pace he can set."

By noon, however, the Sleepers were all gasping for breath. The land had turned uphill, and they seemed headed toward a steep mountain pass.

Beorn's legs were short and stumpy, but he appeared to be as tireless as a machine. He had forged ahead all morning without a single stop, even for a drink.

Now, as the sun was exactly overhead, Josh called out to the dwarf, "Wait a minute. We'll take our noon meal here."

Beorn turned and stared back at him expressionlessly, then shrugged his burly shoulders. He put down his knapsack, opened it, pulled something out, and began to eat.

Sarah was usually the one to see to the meals, and she called to him, "Don't you want to share what we have, Beorn?" She got no answer, and her face reddened. "Well," she said quietly to Abbey as they took food out of their knapsacks, "he doesn't seem to be worried about table manners. Goél certainly has some strange servants."

When they had eaten their cold lunch, Josh said, "We'll make camp tonight in time to have a fire and cook something hot."

Beorn spoke up. "I thought you were in a hurry. Didn't Goél say our journey was urgent?" Finished with his own meal, he was standing impatiently, arms crossed, looking down at the seated Sleepers.

"We'll get there," Josh said grimly. He got up and began repacking his kit. Then, when the others were set, he looked at Beorn. "All right, now we're ready."

All afternoon they trudged uphill. Abbey developed a blister on her heel, and Sarah insisted they stop while she put ointment on it and a tight bandage so that it would not be rubbed even worse.

Abbey bit her lip. "Why does he have to be so mean? We're going as fast as we can."

Reb strolled up to Beorn. "Couldn't you have a little consideration for the ladies? They're not as strong as we are."

Beorn looked the Sleepers over and laughed harshly. "Strong? I don't see anything strong about any of you."

Reb took this as a challenge. "We might be a little bit stronger than you think—some of us."

"You? You're just a *boy.*"

Reb, always sensitive and carrying a bit too much pride, said, "A runt like you shouldn't be too hard to handle."

Beorn grinned. "Why don't you try it?"

Reb put a hand on Beorn's thick chest. He shoved hard, forcing the dwarf one step backward, but he had time to do no more. A steely hand clamped around his wrist. Then he found himself rising in the air and turning a complete somersault. The dwarf tossed him as easily as if he had been stuffed with feathers instead of flesh and blood!

Reb hit the ground, rolled over, and came up spitting dirt. With a wild yell, he charged Beorn, who simply stood waiting.

When the young Southerner was upon him, Beorn shifted quickly, grabbed Reb, and threw him to the ground easily. He held him there while Reb kicked and screamed.

"As I say," Beorn said, "it's up to Goél who goes, but I don't see why he chose a bunch of children for the job."

"Turn him loose!"

Beorn looked up at Glori, standing beside him. Her eyes were half slitted, and she looked very angry.

"Turn him loose, I said!"

Beorn stared at her arrogantly, then slowly nodded. "All right, he's loose."

Reb came to his feet and would have continued the fight, but Glori took his arm. "No, Reb," she said, "this is no time to fight. No one doubts your courage. Dwarfs are known for their brute strength." She glanced at Beorn and sniffed. "They don't have many brains, but they make up for it with brawn."

Beorn simply looked at her, saying nothing. Then he picked up his knapsack, put it on his shoulder, and without another word strode off up the hill.

Reb was trembling with anger and embarrassment.

Wash came up to him. "Never mind, Reb," the small black boy said, slapping his friend on the back. "He's built like a bull. And like Glori says, he doesn't have a lot upstairs, seems like."

"I don't see why Goél had to send *him*," Reb said angrily. "We could've had a map."

"Seems a map would be a lot better than being around *him*, all right."

But Josh called everybody into order, and they followed after the dwarf, who again set an exhausting pace.

That evening, when they made camp, Beorn disappeared for a time. He came back with a rabbit, which he proceeded to roast and then devour without even offering a share to the others.

Later on, when the dwarf was asleep, Glori approached Josh and said quietly, "We have to have a guide, but that one is dangerous."

"What do you mean 'dangerous'?"

"I mean he has no judgment. He's not very bright. He's strong enough and too ignorant to be anything but brave—but that can get us all killed. Be very careful, Josh! That dwarf could lead us all to destruction."

She turned away, and Josh and Sarah stared at each other, considering what Glori had said.

"But we have to follow him," Josh said finally. "He's the only guide we have. And for some reason Goél gave him to us."

"All right, but let's all watch him," Sarah said. "He can get us to the Land of Ice, but after that I don't care if he just disappears and leaves us alone. We have Glori —and she's all we need!"

4
Land of Ice

Josh stumbled along with the other Sleepers. "My feet are frozen stiff!" he moaned. "If I stub my toes one more time, they're going to break off."

All were clothed in furs from head to foot. They wore heavy, fur-lined boots and fur-lined gloves. Still, everyone was shivering and had been for the past three days.

Wash's teeth chattered as he said, "I never *could* stand cold, and this is the coldest place I ever saw. They can have this Land of Ice for all of me."

Beorn had led them over high mountains, across a narrow inlet in boats, and then outfitted them at a village that bordered the icy land where the Aluks lived. The dwarf himself laughed at the cold and at the complaints of the Sleepers. "It'll get worse," he promised. "You'll all be frozen stiff before you get to the Aluks— but I think you'll give up before we get halfway there."

Josh's own lips were stiff with cold, and his nose and cheeks had lost all feeling long ago. "I never knew it'd be like this," he muttered to Sarah, who was walking close by. "I don't see how anybody *lives* in this place." He scanned the long stretches of ice and snow, and his eyes burned in the fierce glare. He took off his gloves in order to rub them.

At once Beorn was at his side. "No! Keep your hands in your gloves, or you'll wind up without any fingers."

"But I can't see. This snow is blinding me."

Beorn stared at him, then nodded. "Then it's time for the glasses."

"You have glasses?"

"I got some at the outpost," Beorn said. "I knew we'd need them." He shifted out of his pack, shuffled through it, and came up with what looked like a girl's hair barrette. He handed the item to Josh. "Put these on."

Josh saw that they were in fact a piece of bone, or horn, in a curved shape. They had thongs that tied behind the head, and across the front was a narrow slit. He fitted them over his ears and at once felt relief.

"Wow," he said, "I can't see as much, but the glare's all gone."

"Everyone put on sunshades," Beorn commanded. "The natives would have been blind a long time ago if they hadn't invented these glasses."

"Pretty smart," Jake said. "I've seen pictures of Eskimos wearing something like this back in Old-world. Does cut down on the vision a little, but at least we can see."

Abbey said, "That *is* better, but I'm so cold, and I'm getting hungry."

"The grub's getting pretty low," Reb said. "We better strike a village pretty soon."

Beorn shook his head. "No village for three days."

"Three days!" Josh cried. "What are we going to eat?"

Beorn did not answer for a moment, then he said, "You wait here. I'll get something to feed you babies." He hefted the harpoon that he had brought from the village. It was a wooden weapon with a barbed tip fastened to the stock. Attached to this was a line of stout cord. Beorn turned without another word and walked off.

"Well, I hope he finds something." Jake shivered. "Let's put up the tents. I wish we had a tree here for firewood."

But there was no tree. There was nothing at all in the waste of ice and snow. Nothing but white as far as the eye could see. Overhead the sky was slate gray, and the sun was almost hidden behind tattered, heavy clouds.

"It's like being under water," Jake complained. "I don't like this place."

None of them liked it and were not likely to like it better.

As they set up camp, Glori said to Abbey, "Have you thought what would happen if Beorn would just leave us here?"

Abbey stared at her in consternation. "Leave us? Why would he do that?"

"He would if he saw a reason. You don't know these dwarfs as I do." She frowned. "They're a stubborn, loveless people. They always think about what's best for *them*. He'd leave us in a minute if something came up that interested him more."

"I can't believe that," Abbey said staunchly.

"And even if he didn't, suppose he fell through the ice." Glori looked around and swept the landscape with a helpless gesture. "Could you find your way back to civilization?"

Fear closed upon Abbey's heart, and she could not answer. For two long hours after that, she kept looking out the tent flap in the direction that Beorn had taken.

Then she saw him. "I see him! He's coming back!"

The Sleepers all rushed out of the tents and watched Beorn's small figure grow larger and larger. He was a moving black spot on the endless white back-

41

ground. When he got closer, they saw that he carried something over his shoulder.

"He's got something to eat!" Abbey said.

Indeed, Beorn tossed a half-grown seal at their feet. "We eat," he said.

Jake said, "I can't eat raw seal." He set up their tiny, single-burner, oil-fed stove and took out their single frying pan. Soon the smell of cooking meat was in the air, and then he was parceling it out.

Beorn, however, laughed at his preparations. "Raw is better," he said. "You cook the good flavor out of it." He was eating a portion of raw seal with a relish that almost turned Abbey's stomach. Even the boys looked a little squeamish.

However, the food seemed to put fresh strength into everyone.

"This will do until we get to the Aluks," Beorn said. He then rolled up in his furs and went to sleep instantly.

"He's like an animal," Sarah whispered. "He can just go to sleep anytime he wants to—or go without sleep forever, it seems like."

"He's tough, and I guess that's one reason Goél sent him," Josh said. "We'd be in a pickle without him out here. I'll just be glad when it's all over."

Three days later the Sleepers, led by the tireless dwarf, were standing in the village of the Aluks.

The chief, a tall, handsome Aluk with coppery skin, a man named Monti, greeted them warmly. He roused the entire village, and the Sleepers were treated royally. They soon learned that Monti was an enthusiastic supporter of Goél. He let them rest for twenty-four hours and then honored them at a banquet, where he pledged his support.

"There are many warriors in other villages. I will send my men out today, and we will all gather and make for the Plains of Dothan at once. We will fight for Goél."

This was encouraging news to Josh.

Although Monti urged the Sleepers to stay and rest, Josh shook his head, saying, "No, chief, we must go now to the Land of the Centaurs."

They stayed one more day only. Then, carrying as much dried food in their packs as they could walk with, they were led out, once again, by Beorn.

A vicious snowstorm delayed them, but Beorn promised, "Three more days, and no more snow."

"That'll be a relief," Josh said, and the others heartily agreed.

Reb had been sullen and angry with Beorn ever since their scuffle. But as they tramped along the next day, Beorn suddenly turned to him and said, "You would make a good dwarf."

Reb stared at him. "I'd rather be anything than a dwarf."

"You're a tough man. I take back what I said about you," Beorn said. "I admire courage and toughness. All dwarfs honor those things." Then Beorn turned and walked away.

Reb looked at Abbey. "What do you think of that?"

"I think he was making some kind of an apology."

"It's the first kind word he's said to *anybody*. I didn't know he had it in him."

"I think the dwarfs are just like that. They're probably warm and loving to each other."

"I doubt that." Reb grinned. "I bet that in their courtship the men and women beat up on each other with sticks."

"You're impossible, Reb! There's not a romantic bone in your body."

"Well, you've got enough romantic bones for the whole crew." He felt better, however, and later told Josh, "I guess the dwarf is all right. Just a little bit hard to get to know."

"He's tough enough, that's for sure. And that's a good thing for us."

Half an hour later, Josh found out exactly how tough Beorn was. They were trudging along through light snow when suddenly, out of nowhere, a monstrous white form rose up. The only color he saw was the red roof of its gaping mouth.

"Polar bear!" Josh screamed. He fumbled with numb hands for the sword at his side. *We're dead this time!* he thought, knowing that a puny sword would never stop that monster. But he managed to cry, "Weapons out!"

All of them pulled their swords, and Glori fumbled for the bow strapped to her back. They watched openmouthed as the bear pounded toward them. It was at least twice as big as any Oldworld bear. Its beady black eyes gleamed.

He must weigh a thousand pounds! Josh thought with astonishment. He was running forward, sword at the ready, but he still feared that the mighty creature would not be slowed by the sword of any man.

Crouched between the Sleepers and the bear, Beorn gripped his harpoon in both hands.

There was no place to run, and Beorn well knew the power of a bear's slashing talons. *He'll have one chance*, Josh thought. *And one only.* Beorn would also well know that the bear's muscular body was so tough that a harpoon, even if it penetrated its chest, would

44

not stop the charge. *It must strike in the open mouth —right up through the brain.*

The bear's feet slapped the snow in a relentless *slap, slap, slap.* He loomed larger and larger, charging straight at the hunching dwarf.

He hasn't got a chance, Josh thought desperately as he moved up behind Beorn. *None of us do.*

The bear now was hardly ten feet away. Beorn lunged forward, his full weight behind the blow. The bear's mouth was open, saliva on its red tongue, huge teeth curving inward. Straight toward that target, the open red mouth, Beorn drove the barbed end of the harpoon.

His aim was accurate. The mighty beast met the weapon at full speed. Beorn's feet were planted when the harpoon penetrated—but then the weight of the bear struck him. He was thrown high into the air, then hit the ice, where he rolled over and over and over. The harpoon had been ripped out of his hands.

The bear rolled too, clawing at the harpoon that extended out of its mouth. But the barb had pierced the skull, and, after a few feeble motions, the monster lay dead.

Beorn came to his feet, took one look, and gave a victory cry. *"Aaiiii,* I have killed you, my friend!"

"Beorn!" Josh shouted.

All of the Sleepers crowded around the dwarf.

"Beorn, you're wounded!" Abbey said.

The bear's talons had ripped the front of the dwarf's furs. Abbey pulled them back to reveal great bloody furrows across his muscular brown chest. "Quick!" she said. "We've got to do something. Those are terrible wounds."

Beorn stared at her. "They are not bad."

"They're *terrible!* And everybody knows animal

45

claws will cause infection. We've got to treat these wounds right now!"

They put up one tent and got Beorn inside, where Abbey took charge. She was actually very good with minor injuries—but Josh knew she had never seen wounds like these. She said, "We'll have to wash these with disinfectant. Then we'll have to sew up the worst ones."

"Have you ever done that, Abbey?" Josh whispered.

"No, but somebody's got to do it. Do you want to try it?"

"Not me!"

None of the others volunteered, and it was Abbey who took some gut thread and a crude needle from the kit that the dwarf himself carried.

The dwarf murmured, "Flask in my sack."

Reb found the flask in the dwarf's sack and brought it back.

Beorn took the top off the flask and turned it up. The liquid gurgled as he swallowed it, and Josh smelled the scent of alcohol.

Five minutes after he had taken this, Beorn was practically unconscious.

Abbey bent to her task, her lips set and her eyes determined. She sewed together the worst of the cuts and bound Beorn's chest with underclothing ripped into bandages. When she had finished, she said shakily, "I don't know how I did it—but I guess you do what you have to do."

"We won't be traveling very fast now," Josh said. "And we can't go on at all until he's able to travel, and that'll be a week."

They were mistaken, however. The next day Beorn sat up and said, "We travel now."

46

"No," Abbey said, "*not* now. You'll pull those stitches out. We'll wait until tomorrow at least."

Beorn stared at her but then agreed. "You are a good seamstress," he said. He pulled his furs to one side and looked down at his chest. "Very neat."

Actually they had to wait two days, and even then Beorn was not able to carry his pack. They divided his kit among themselves.

Beorn led the way, however. They made slow time, but three days later he pointed forward to a thin line of dark mountains. "There—no more ice. We can get rid of these furs. And the tents."

"That'll be a relief," Dave said. He was carrying most of Beorn's supplies because he was the largest and the strongest. "I'll be glad to see the last of this territory."

That night Abbey, who was wakeful, found Beorn staring into the campfire. "I need to change that bandage, Beorn," she told him.

Beorn nodded and slipped off his fur top. He watched the girl's face as she undid the bandages and put fresh ones on.

"Why are you looking at me like that?" she asked.

"Why are you doing this for me?"

"I'd do it for anyone. Besides, you're one of us."

The idea seemed novel to Beorn. He was quiet for a long time after putting his furs back on. "No, I'm not one of you. I'm not one of anyone."

"What about your family?"

"They were killed by the Dark Lord. My wife and my three children."

The starkness of his reply caused Abbey to open her eyes wide. "Oh, I'm so sorry," she said and put a hand on his arm.

Beorn looked down at her hand. "You are kind. I wish I were kind. Always I'm angry."

Later Abbey told Josh, "No wonder he's surly—he's lost everything he loved. Now he lives only to fight the Dark Lord."

"I feel bad," Josh said. "We haven't been all that friendly to him. I guess we never understand why other people act the way they do."

Two days later the ice began to break up into hard ground—rock at first, then soil. Then trees appeared, and Josh said, "We're out of it at last. I hope we don't have as much trouble finding the centaurs as we did getting out of Aluk land."

"We won't. I know the way there," Glori said. "In fact, I don't think you need stay with us, Beorn, if you want to return to your tribe."

"No," Josh said instantly. "We do need him." He reached over suddenly and slapped Beorn on the back. "You saved our bacon with that bear! There wouldn't be any of us here if it weren't for you. No, Beorn's one of us—he stays to the end."

A strange light glittered in the dark eyes of the dwarf. His lips relaxed from their tense lines into a smile, and he said, "I will go with you. All the way."

Glori took over the leadership. As Goél had said, she had traveled to the Land of the Centaurs before. They made better time now, and Beorn continued to heal more quickly than anyone had thought possible. When the weather grew milder, they discarded the furs with relief and left the tents behind.

As he put on more comfortable clothes, Wash said, "I hope I never have to put on a fur coat again!"

"Me too." Reb clapped his Stetson back on his

head. "And I wish I had me a hoss to ride." He still had his lasso, however. "You just let a reindeer or something go by—anything with four legs—and I'll rope it. Then me and you'll ride, Josh."

They were not, however, to do anything like that, for on the second day after Glori took over, disaster struck.

They were walking cheerfully along in a valley, talking and laughing, when suddenly Josh stumbled and coughed.

Sarah, walking beside him, turned to see what was wrong. "Josh—" she began, and then she froze in horror—an arrow had been driven through Josh's shoulder!

"*Josh!*" And then she heard the cries of warriors. Quickly looking upward, she saw a band of men armed with bows lining the top of the ravine.

Arrows began to fly. Sarah saw one scrape Jake's leg.

Reb cried, "We've got to get out of here! They've got us pinned down."

At that moment a unit of soldiers clad in leather armor and armed with swords pounced out from behind the clump of bushes straight ahead.

It was Beorn who met them, giving his war cry. He swung his battle-ax left and right, but he was driven back.

Reb and Dave and Jake battled with their swords as Glori and the girls fitted arrows to their bows.

Sarah nocked an arrow and targeted a warrior who was coming at her with sword swinging wildly. He went down, and she fitted another arrow, but she soon saw that the swordsmen were too many for them. Their number was overwhelming.

"Back!" Beorn said. "Retreat!"

Sarah felt the dwarf's hands on her. She resisted, crying, "We can't leave Josh!" But she had no chance against Beorn's strength.

They fought a retreat, and it was the arrows of the girls that finally discouraged pursuit.

They paused to draw breath in a grove of trees, and Reb looked down at a ragged cut across his palm. He took out his handkerchief, wound the cloth around it, and said slowly, "They got Josh."

"We've got to go back and get him!" Sarah said.

Glori said at once, "Yes, we must counterattack. Everyone get ready."

Beorn shook his head. "No. We must not go back. There are too many of them."

"But we can't leave *Josh* there," Sarah pleaded. "Beorn, we've *got* to get him."

Beorn shook his head again, fiercely. "We have a mission for Goél. If we go back, we'll *all* be taken. Then who'll carry out Goél's orders?"

A fierce debate arose.

Glori said, "You may be a coward, Beorn, but the rest of us are not! We're going back to fight and rescue Josh."

Beorn stared at her. "You are wrong," he said quietly, his guttural voice very deep in his chest. "If we go back, we cannot win. Then Goél's mission will not be carried out."

Glori won the debate; but as it turned out, Beorn was right. They made a futile attack. The enemy swarms were too great. Every Sleeper was wounded and driven back.

Even Sarah saw that it was hopeless. She had taken an arrow in the calf of her leg, and the pain was excruciating, but she could only think, *They've got Josh. They'll kill him.*

Beorn squatted down beside her and put a hand on her shoulder. "I know how you feel," he said quietly. "I, too, have lost the ones I loved."

Sarah looked up, her eyes brimming. She could not say a word. No matter how this battle turned out, she had lost. Without Josh, Nuworld was not the place that it had been.

"We must go on," Glori announced loudly.

Jake looked at her, almost with anger. "Your idea didn't work too well. Now all of us are shot up, and we still don't have Josh."

Beorn said at once, "Let us not fight among ourselves. We must go to the Land of the Centaurs. That is the command of Goél." His eyes narrowed, and he murmured in Sarah's hearing, "But how did they find us—those soldiers of the Dark Lord? How did they find us?"

"Maybe they just happened on us by chance," she said.

"No, I don't think so. I think they were sent to this place." A heavy expression came into his dark eyes. Then he said, "We must be watchful, Sarah. The way before us is dangerous, and we are weak."

He turned away, and his powerful shoulders drooped as though they bore a burden.

5

Caverns of Doom

Wash could not remember the Sleepers ever being so spiritless and unhappy as they all were on their retreat from the battle with the servants of the Dark Lord.

As they made their way through a mountain pass, still marching steadily upward, Jake remarked, "I might as well tell you, Wash. I'm in a blue funk."

Wash gave him a sober look. "I don't know what a blue funk is, but if it means being totally miserable—then I've got it too." He lifted his eyes to where Glori led the way, then glanced backward to Beorn, who was protecting the rear of their small column. "Ever since we lost Josh," he said mournfully, "I don't care whether school keeps or not."

"Me either," Jake said, his face grim. "I feel we failed him somehow."

"We did the best we could," Wash said defensively. "There just wasn't enough of us to go back and rescue him." He hesitated, then tried to be more cheerful. "He'll be all right. At least he's alive."

"We don't know that."

"He was when we last saw him. He took an arrow in the shoulder. But it wasn't enough to kill him."

"You know the Dark Lord's methods better than that," Jake snorted. "They'll pull him apart muscle by muscle if they decide to, trying to get information out of him."

Wash did not answer. He knew that, indeed, Jake

53

spoke the truth. The Dark Lord's captains had no mercy, and Wash tried not to think what a terrible time Josh Adams might be going through.

Abbey fell into step with Sarah. She knew that Sarah, of all the Sleepers, was hardest hit by what had happened to Josh. Sarah and Josh had been the closest of friends, and now the sun had gone out of her sky. As they retreated into the dark mountains away from their pursuers, she seemed unable to find a single spot of joy.

Abbey was silent for a time, yearning to give her some comfort. Finally she said, "We mustn't give up. We've been in tough spots before, Sarah."

Sarah blinked the tears away before she could say, "I'm trying to keep hoping, but it's hard, Abbey!"

Abbey trudged along beside the older girl but could think of no comforting words. Glancing over her shoulder, she said, "Beorn thinks that they're going to catch up with us." At this point, Abbey thought, Sarah probably didn't care, though she was visibly trying to keep up a good front before the others.

"I know he does," Sarah said wearily. Looking at the craggy rocks on each side of them and the narrow trail ahead, growing steeper with every mile, she said, "I don't know how long we can keep up this pace. All of us got hurt. My leg's killing me." She looked down to where blood had soaked through the bandage around her calf.

"We mustn't let that get infected. And you really need to rest."

"I don't think there's any hope of that. Beorn says we've got to keep going or we'll get trapped."

All morning long they plodded upward. The air seemed thinner now. At one place the going grew so steep that Abbey said, "Beorn, we've *got* to rest. Besides, Sarah's bandage needs changing, and so does yours."

Beorn came back and glanced at Sarah's leg. "All right," he agreed, "we'll take a break. But we can't stop long."

Abbey quickly assumed her role as nurse. She put more antiseptic on Sarah's wound and commented that it looked inflamed. She rebandaged it, rebandaged Beorn's chest, and washed the soiled wrappings in a stream for future use. Then she went around treating the others, who had taken minor scratches. The only medication she had was the bottle of antiseptic, growing dangerously low.

As Abbey treated injuries, Beorn drew Dave to one side, looking back down the path.

"They're there," he said grimly.

"Have you seen them?"

"Yes, even though they're clever at concealing themselves. And I think they know these mountains better than I do."

"Glori says we'll be all right if we can make it through this pass."

Beorn did not answer. His dark eyes were fixed on the canyon below. Suddenly he exclaimed, "There! I saw them that time."

"How many? Can you tell?"

"No, it's too far, but a half dozen could pin us down and starve us out." He gnawed his lip and ran a hand through his black hair. "I don't know how we're going to make it through," he finally said, his voice filled with defeat. "But we've got to!"

"If we don't get through," Dave exclaimed, "the centaurs and the magicians won't be alerted. Goél told

Josh they were very important—almost vital—to the last battle."

"He told me the same thing." He looked up at the boy and said with surprising gentleness, "You miss your friend Josh."

"Yes, I do. We've been together a long time. We haven't always gotten along, but he's my friend. I wish we could go back and get him. Oh, I know we can't," he said hurriedly, holding up a hand. "All I can hope is that he's all right. And that somehow we'll be able to get him back from those people."

"It looks like they're more apt to get us than we are to get him." Then Beorn's eyes flashed. "There—did you see that?"

"Yes, it was the sun on a shield or spear, wasn't it?"

"They're coming up. We'll have to go on even if Sarah is hurting."

They hurried back to the others, and Beorn looked at Glori defiantly. "We've got to move."

"Sarah's not able to travel," she said coldly.

"She won't be any better if the Dark Lord's henchmen get their hands on her. That leg wound will be nothing compared to what they'll do to her."

The coldness between the two, which had always lain just beneath the surface, was now out in the open.

Glori said, "You were the leader to the Land of Ice, Beorn, but the Sleepers must follow me now. Either take my orders or leave!"

Beorn said nothing. He settled himself back on his heels and glared at her. He knew what Goél had said. Until now, it had been his task to guide the Sleepers— but she knew these mountains, and he did not.

"What should we do, Glori?" Reb asked.

"Just try to lose them. I know a pass up ahead. We

may be able to take that, and maybe they'll lose us. Can you walk, Sarah?"

"I can make it." Sarah painfully got to her feet.

Beorn thought she was trying not to let the pain show on her face.

The little procession wound upward, all stumbling as they went. Two long hours later, Glori led them off the main trail.

"Wait! I know this part of the trail at least!" Beorn said. "It's a dead end."

"I know a way out."

Beorn tried to argue, but Glori said sharply, "Be quiet, Beorn. We haven't got time to discuss it. Just follow me!"

Wearily they forged forward for another hour until they came up against a solid rock wall that barred their path.

"We can't climb that!" Dave exclaimed. He turned to Glori.

She gnawed her lip. "I must've taken a wrong turn," she said.

Beorn looked back down the path. "Those men are trackers. They'll find us here. They're probably right on our heels, so we can't go back the way we came."

All the Sleepers appeared overcome with dismay.

Sarah slumped to the ground, as though her wounded leg was unable to bear her weight. "What can we do? We're too weak to fight. We've got to hide."

"Hide *where?*" Jake demanded. He looked up at the sheer wall. "There's no way to go but back."

"That won't do," Beorn said. "Those trackers are on their way to this spot right now."

But Glori said, "We'll *have* to go back. There's no other choice. Maybe they missed our tracks."

"No," Beorn said slowly, "there *is* another way out." When they all stared at him in shock, he said, "I recognize this place. I was here only once before, and it was many years ago, but I do remember this one spot." His dark eyes glowed with sudden fire. "We can go through the Caverns of Doom."

The very sound of Beorn's words visibly sent a chill through every Sleeper.

"The Caverns of Doom!" Wash exclaimed. "That don't sound like nothin' I want to go through."

"We can't go through that place!" Glori exclaimed.

"Have you ever been there?" Beorn demanded.

"Of course not! No one goes there—except renegade dwarfs." She turned to the Sleepers. "The Caverns of Doom are caves made partly by nature, and they became the home of wicked dwarfs."

"They were not *wicked!*" Beorn cried. "They were my forefathers, and that was their home until the Dark Lord sent traitors among us."

"I won't argue about it," Glori said. "We're not going through the Caverns of Doom!"

"Wait a minute, Glori," Dave said suddenly. He cast a wary glance at the path they had taken to this dead end. "We've got to do *something*. Is it really a dangerous place, Beorn?"

Beorn did not answer for a moment. Then he said, "Yes, it is dangerous. Foul things lurk there these days —and underground rivers that could sweep us away. But I say *that* danger is not so great as falling into the hands of the Dark Lord. I would throw myself off a cliff before I would be captured by him!"

Another debate followed then. Glori firmly argued that it would be suicide to go into the Caverns of Doom. Beorn stubbornly urged that it was their only hope.

Finally Jake declared, "Look, *I'm* not going to be caught by those fellows back there. They'd have us in the torture chamber in the Dread Tower before it was over. I vote for the Caverns."

"So do I," Abbey said, surprising Beorn. He'd thought her a timid girl, but apparently she had been given courage for this.

She came and put a hand on his shoulder. He was shorter than she and, of course, much wider. Summoning up a smile, she said, "I'll trust you, Beorn. Do you know the way?"

"If you vote to go, I will do my best to bring you through safely," Beorn said simply.

Immediately Reb said, "I'm for the Caverns. Let's get going."

"Me too," Dave said, and Wash quickly echoed his vote. That left it up to Sarah, who rose with a grimace of pain. "Yes, I'll try anything to stay out of their hands."

Glori glared at the Sleepers. "It is the wrong thing to do," she said, "but I vowed to Goél to do my best for you. So I will go—though we all go to our deaths."

"We do not know that," Beorn said. His eyes glowed with eagerness. "I know the Caverns will be dangerous, but Goél will be with us, and I think I remember the way. Come—there is a hidden entrance."

For the next half hour they scrambled through broken rock along the cliff wall until they reached a small valley.

"Here," Beorn said. "Just as I remember. The entrance is right behind that big boulder."

"We can't move that!" Dave exclaimed. "It's too big."

"It's balanced," Beorn said. "Look!" He stood under the rock and braced his back against it. Shoving with both of his powerful legs and grunting, he rolled the stone to one side.

"There," he said, panting. He motioned to the mouth of an exposed cave. "Get your torches ready. We will burn only one at a time to make sure that they last. Everyone stay as close to me as you can. Dave, you bring up the rear. We go for Goél," Beorn said. Then he plunged into the dark cavern.

At first the blackness in the Caverns seemed as thick as the surrounding rock out of which they were carved. Only the flickering light of the torch held aloft by Beorn lit the way. However, Sarah, who followed immediately behind him, discovered that after a time her eyes adjusted to the intense dark. The pathway was wide and flat, as if beaten by many feet. Above, the cave roof arched upward nearly ten feet at the highest point.

Beorn gave them an encouraging word from time to time. When they came to a fork, he said, "I remember. That way—" he motioned to the right "—leads to a trap. No one comes out again from that passage."

"Are you sure it's the *right* one that's the trap?" Glori asked. She stared into both darkened ways and appeared unhappy about the whole thing. "It's not too late to turn back . . ."

"We can't do that," Sarah said wearily. "Go on, Beorn."

Beorn plunged down the left passageway.

The cavern trail gradually began to lead downward. Sarah felt the tilt of the path beneath her feet. Down, down, down they went. Then she began hearing the gurgle of an underground river, and finally they came to it. Fortunately the stream was very narrow.

"We must fill up our canteens here," Beorn said,

"and drink all we can. I'm not sure when we will find water again."

They rested for a while and ate a little. Then Beorn said, "Now we will enter the real dwarf country."

"I'm not sure I *want* to go into the dwarf country," Reb muttered. He glanced around. He was next in line in front of Dave. Then he reached forward and tapped Wash on the shoulder. "Don't you get lost. With your coloration it would be easy, and we'd never find you."

Wash turned and grinned, his teeth flashing. "Maybe you better tie a string on me, Reb."

"I don't know about all this," Jake muttered. "I never did like underground stuff."

"It reminds me of the Underworld," Abbey murmured. "I wish we had some of our friends from there to guide us."

On and on they went until exhaustion compelled them to stop. They sat down to rest, and Sarah and Abbey worked on preparing food. They had bits of cold meat left and some dried fruit that was almost unchewable, but they made the best of it.

Beorn insisted they keep only one torch burning, saving the others for later. "Plenty of air in here," he said. "See how the flame burns?" Then he waved an arm. "I remember this place. It was a big conference room in the old days."

Then they pulled out their sleeping bags.

"Hard to know if it's sleep time when you don't know whether it's day or night," Wash muttered to Reb, who lay only a few feet away.

"Don't matter to me," Reb said cheerfully. "Day or night, I'm sleepy. Sleep when I'm sleepy, drink when I'm dry. That's what I do."

Several hours later, Beorn roused them.

"I don't think they would dare follow us down here," he said, "but we can't take the chance," he said. "Reb, you be the rearguard now. From time to time, stop and listen. Call out if you hear anything coming up behind us."

"All right, Beorn. If they followed us into the cave, I just hope they took that other fork. We don't need any battles in here."

They trudged on.

At last Beorn announced, "This is one of the lowest levels of the Caverns of Doom."

"We haven't seen any monsters," Wash said, looking around nervously. "Maybe they've all left."

Beorn shook his head in denial. "They are here. And we must be very careful. Not all our enemies are human."

He did not elaborate, but just his words were enough to frighten Sarah. She could imagine the horrible things that might lurk underground here—huge worms with sharp teeth and other sorts of terrible monsters. They encountered nothing, however.

And then they came to another decision point. The cavern broke off once more into two wings. One passageway led upward; the other led down.

Glori said, "I've heard tales of this place. That is the doorway to the deepest part of the Caverns of Doom." She pointed to the downward passage. "We don't want to go there."

"Yes, we do," Beorn said. "That way—" he pointed upward "—is where the Dark Lord will have his men stationed. They know we came into the Caverns, and they'll be waiting for us when we come out. We must go down deeper."

Sarah, who by now had a slight fever, could not

understand most of the debate that ensued. Eventually she heard somebody say, "We'll have to take a vote."

It was Jake's voice. "How many of you vote to go down the way Beorn says?" he asked.

Only Abbey raised her hand.

Jake said regretfully, "Well, Beorn, it looks like you're outvoted this time. I think we've had all we can take of these tunnels."

Beorn shook his head stubbornly. "To go upward is a mistake."

"No, it is not!" Glori exclaimed. "We'll die if we go down farther. Come on, everyone. We've got to get out of this horrible pit!"

Sarah saw Abbey move next to Beorn.

"I'm sorry," Abbey said to him. "I did all I could. Everybody's just so tired and half sick. They've got to have light."

Beorn did not answer her. Looking toward the trail that led upward, he sighed. "Sometimes the easy way will prove to be the hardest." There was a note of gloom in his voice. As they started forward and upward, he loosened his battle-ax, and his eyes gleamed in the semidarkness.

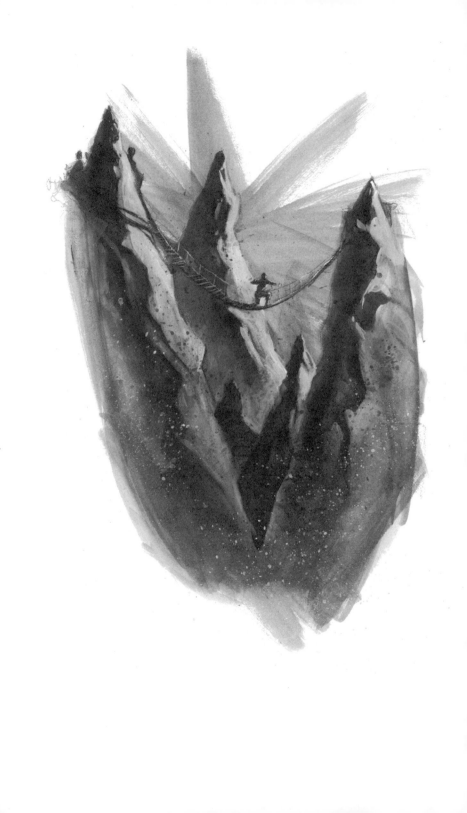

6

A Fearful Loss

Somehow the very act of heading upward, where they knew there were light and fresh air, encouraged the Sleepers.

Wash said, "It was just like going down into your grave when we kept going downhill into that tunnel!"

Beorn said nothing as they trudged upward. He kept his battle-ax unsheathed though, and his eyes were constantly looking ahead.

And then they came to a chasm so deep that the light of Glori's torch would not permit them to see the bottom.

"I'd hate to fall into that sucker!" Reb whistled softly. He picked up a stone, tossed it over, counted off the seconds, which seemed forever, and finally he heard a faint *clink* as the stone hit. "Nope—" he shook his head violently "—let's not fall into there."

"This way." Glori held the torch forward.

She was standing on the very brink, and Reb came alongside to peer into the gloom ahead. "Are we supposed to cross on *that?*" he exclaimed.

What he saw was a fragile bridge that had been constructed across the chasm. It looked so tiny that when Jake joined them he said, "I wouldn't trust that thing for my cat to walk across!"

"It will be safe enough. We will go one at a time," Glori announced. To show her confidence, she strode out onto the bridge and stood in the middle of it. "You see? Just come singly. It's stronger than it looks." Then she crossed to the other side and stood waiting, encouraging them to make the trip.

One by one they crossed over.

Glori smiled. "Now, from here on it will be better, I trust."

"That wasn't much of a bridge," Reb grumbled. "They make better bridges than that back where I come from."

The Sleepers and the dwarf hurried after Glori as she led them ever upward. The tunnel twisted this way and that, and soon everyone was exclaiming over the breath of fresh air that struck them.

"I think I see light up ahead!" Sarah cried.

Reb strained to see, and, sure enough, he could make out a pinpoint of light.

Glori laughed. "See? I told you this was the way to come."

She quickened her pace, the others stumbling after her. The pinpoint of light grew, and then they were almost at the cave entrance.

"Wait!" Beorn commanded gutturally. "Don't go out there yet!"

"You stay in your caverns if you want," Glori said coldly. "The rest of us need sunlight."

She stepped outside into a wooded area, and the Sleepers crowded after her. Reb was almost blinded by the brightness, and he half shut his eyes as he tried to look around.

"This way," Glori said. "The trail is plain."

"Just a minute," Dave said. "I thought I saw something . . ."

"What is it, Dave?" Sarah asked.

"I thought I saw sunlight reflecting on some metal."

"There's no *metal* up here in these woods!" Jake exclaimed. "Wait, I see it too." Then he cried, "Look out, here they come! They found us!"

Instantly the air was filled with flying arrows. The Sleepers stumbled back into the shelter of the cavern, and Beorn cried, "The rest of you—take the torch and go back! I will hold them here at the entrance."

"I'll stay and help you," Dave said firmly.

"I'm staying too!" Jake said, his jaw pushed out in a daring way.

"So am I," Reb said. "Wash, take the girls back. Look after them. We'll give you a chance to get across the bridge."

Wash didn't want to leave them, Reb could tell. But he obeyed, and the other three Sleepers and Glori —and the torch—quickly disappeared back down into the cavern.

Beorn said, "Four for one then." He smiled crook-edly. "We have some advantage—the warriors won't be able to use their bows as well in here. And they'll be blinded by the darkness."

The four defenders stood shoulder to shoulder in the darkness. Soon they heard voices. And then they saw that they did have the advantage, for they could see their enemies against the light of the cave opening. Those who came at them could see nothing.

They heard the hissing of Beorn's battle-ax, though, and felt the slashes of the swords wielded by Dave and Reb and Jake. Shrill cries went up until, it seemed, the warriors could not be urged further into the blackness to face unseen death.

"Now," said Beorn, "we go."

The defenders slowly gave way, leaving their at-tackers—many fallen—behind them. They groped their way back down the unlit tunnel to the bridge, where they found the others on the far side, waiting with the welcome torch.

When the four had crossed, Beorn began hacking at the timbers that held the bridge in place. His sharp ax made the chips fly.

Glori said, "If you destroy the bridge, we can't get back across!"

"And they can't get at us!" Beorn answered grimly. Soon the bridge sagged, then with a crash ripped loose from its moorings. It fell into the cavernous depths, turning slowly, and made a tremendous smash at the bottom of the cavern.

"Now we go back," Beorn said. He stared at Glori as if awaiting a challenge, but she said nothing.

"Just a minute," Wash whispered. "I . . . I don't think I can make it . . ." And he collapsed.

"Wash!" Reb cried. "What's the matter? Bring the light over here!"

Reb leaned over him. "He's taken an arrow!"

The arrow was a short, stubby one, more a dart than an arrow, but it had pierced Wash's side. Abbey tried to stem the severe bleeding.

Wash, however, whispered, "No, you've . . . got to go on!"

"Wash," Reb said, his voice breaking, "you'll be all right."

Wash reached up a hand feebly, and Reb grabbed it with both of his. "You're gonna have to go on . . . without me," Wash said, his voice growing weaker.

Beorn said nothing, for this was a matter for the Sleepers. He and Glori stood back while Dave, Reb, Jake, and the two girls gathered around the injured boy. His head was in Sarah's lap now, and he was speaking so faintly that they had to lean close to hear.

"Looks like . . . I won't be . . . at the last battle," he

68

whispered, "but you guys have got to make it. Don't worry . . . about leaving me here . . . I'll see you . . . again."

"Wash," Reb said, "you can't die!" Tears were running down his cheeks. He held the hand of the small boy tightly. "You just can't, Wash."

"You been . . . my best friend, Reb," Wash whispered. He looked around and said, "All of you . . . my good friends." He closed his eyes, and they thought he was gone, but he opened them and said more strongly. "We've had . . . a good time." He took each hand, then closed his eyes again as one who was weary from long labor. "I wish . . . I could be at the end . . . with you. But Goél . . . he'll look out for us all."

Silence filled the tunnel, and then Abbey sobbed, "He's gone! Wash—Wash is gone!"

They looked at one another.

"We can't take him with us," Sarah whispered.

"This will be his burial ground," Beorn said suddenly, his voice deep, his eyes brooding. "It is a grave for a valiant warrior. No one will disturb him here."

And so it was. They had no choice. Beorn found a small alcove, and there they placed the body. Afterward, each Sleeper said his good-bye to the small, still form. Then they turned away, eyes blinded with tears, and Beorn closed the alcove opening with stones.

On the way leading back down to the deepest parts of the Caverns of Doom, Sarah said brokenly, "Josh and now Wash—both gone! No matter what happens, things will never be the same again!"

7

The Centaurs

Beorn conducted the Sleepers and Glori deep into the bowels of the earth where they traveled for what seemed hours. But at last they emerged into the world of sunlight and fresh air without meeting further opposition. They knew that the soldiers of the Dark Lord behind them had been cut off by the chasm they could not cross over.

Now they were passing through a golden grassy plain. Herds of Nuworld cattle grazed here and there and lifted their heads to look curiously at the band that forged through their fields. The Sleepers were all limping badly.

"How much farther is it?" Dave asked Glori, who had resumed her place as guide.

"Do you see that low ridge ahead—the one that looks like a smudge on the horizon?" She pointed. "That is the home of the centaurs. We should be there tomorrow."

Jake looked across the enormous distance and groaned. "I've about worn my shoe leather off," he complained, "but let's keep going if we have to."

There was an unhappy note in his voice, but he trudged on. After a time he noticed that Reb had fallen far behind. This was unusual, for the Southern boy usually was as far in advance of the party as possible. Slowing his steps, Jake waited until Reb was even with him, then said, "I don't feel like going much of anywhere. Do you, Reb?"

"No."

Jake waited for Reb to continue, and when he saw that Reb's lips were pressed firmly together, he thought, *He's grieving over Wash. Those two were closer than brothers.* Aloud he said gently, "It's rough. First Josh, and now Wash."

Reb did not reply for a time. The only sounds were the cries of a few birds overhead and the fall of their footsteps as they plodded through the field.

"It's like I lost an arm," Reb said finally, pain etched on his face. "For two years now, we've hardly been separated at all. I got so that I sort of thought like Wash did, and he thought like I did."

Jake knew better than to speak of their loss again.

The sun was just beginning to fall toward the west when Beorn said loudly, "Look!"

All of them lifted their heads to see what appeared to be a band of horsemen coming directly toward them.

"I hope they're friendly," Glori said uneasily. "We're trapped out in the open—we wouldn't have a chance if they decided to make a fight of it."

Sarah, whose eyesight was keener than most, was staring. She said with shock, "Those aren't men on horses!"

"What?" Dave shaded his eyes with a hand and waited for a moment. "You're right," he said. "I never saw anything like that!"

By this time, others could see more clearly the group that was approaching. Abbey whispered, "I knew we were coming to the Land of the Centaurs, but I guess I never really expected that they'd look like *that.*"

To Sarah, however, they looked exactly as she had pictured them. There were eight of them. All had the bodies of fine horses. One was white, three were black, one was a bay color, one looked like a pinto, and two were palomino, a light cream.

But there their similarity to horses ended. Rising out of the front quarters of each one, instead of the arching neck and fine head of a horse, was the body of a man. All were deeply muscled, the kind of development she had seen in weight lifters and acrobats back in Oldworld. Every muscle stood out clearly. Most had long hair that whipped back in the breeze. They carried powerful bows and wore quivers of arrows over their backs. Their faces were stern and noble.

The leader was the strongest-looking of all. The horse part of him was cream colored, and his hair was a rich auburn, slightly curly and tied in the back with a leather thong. His voice boomed, "Who are you, and what is your business in the Land of the Centaurs?"

The centaurs surrounded the travelers and nocked arrows to their bowstrings.

Reb stared about and said, "I feel like we're in the covered-wagon days and the Comanches are surrounding us. Boy, I never seen anything like this!"

"You ought to like it, Reb," Dave murmured. "You always loved horses. This is what you should have been—one of these fellas."

Glori was holding up both hands in a sign of peace. "Hold your hands up, everyone!" she directed the Sleepers. "We come in peace," she cried to the centaurs. "These are the Sleepers, sent by Goél to speak with Aramore, your chief."

The centaur leader released his bowstring and replaced the arrow in his quiver. He trotted forward and examined them with clear gray eyes. There was a kind of nobility about him as he said, "My name is

Moonwise. I am captain of the Armies of the Centaurs. We have heard of the Sleepers. You are the Seven?"

"The dwarf and I are merely guides," Glori answered. "These are five of the Sleepers."

"Where are the other two?" Moonwise demanded.

Glori answered slowly, "They have been lost on the way. Victims of the Dark Lord."

Moonwise considered her words, then looked into the faces of the newcomers. He moved about slowly, so that he could stare at each one, and each felt the impact of his powerful scrutiny.

He paused last by Sarah, and his gaze seemed to reach down into her very depths. He said nothing, but Sarah knew that somehow he was aware of her grief.

Moonwise nodded slowly. "I welcome you to our land. I will take you to Aramore, our chief."

"Most of us are tired," Glori said. "Some have been wounded."

"You shall not walk," Moonwise said. He turned to Sarah. "Come, get on my back, and I will bear your burden."

Sarah swallowed hard, but determination came to her. She moved to the huge horse-man and looked up at him. He replaced the bow over his shoulder, then bent over to pick her up as if she had no weight at all. He swung her around and onto his wide, strong back, saying gently, "Hold onto me so that you will not fall off. We will not go fast, however."

"Yes, Moonwise," Sarah whispered. She put her arms around the powerful body and held on tightly.

The others were selected by the remaining centauri. When one of the black-bodied horse-men came to Beorn, the dwarf shook his head. "Dwarfs do not ride."

"You will ride this time," the centaur said. And he reached down and picked up Beorn. The dwarf seemed

74

shocked at the ease with which the centaur placed him in the center of his back.

"Hang on," the centaur said. "Dwarfs take orders from the centauri in this land." His blue eyes gleamed. "When I come underground to your home below the earth, then *you* may give the orders. What is your name?"

"Beorn."

"My name is Skyfill. Welcome to our country."

All were mounted by now, and Reb, who rode a centaur named Clemore, was delighted. "I rode lots of horses," he said, "but I never had anything like this happen."

"Do you like horses?" his centaur asked.

"Yes, I do. I like 'em better than most people do."

The centaur twisted around to look into Reb's eyes. A smile came to his lips. "I trust that you will always respect centaurs."

At a word from Moonwise, the troop broke into a gallop.

Even Abbey, never an expert horsewoman, apparently found it easy to stay on the back of her centaur. His gallop was smooth, and she had her arms around his powerful waist. He had brown curly hair that flew back into her face. She held on tightly, watching the land fly by.

The centaurs' powerful hooves churned up chunks of dirt as they sped across the fields without ceasing. For an hour they did not diminish their speed, yet showed no signs of tiring.

And then Moonwise cried out, "There is our city!"

It was a strange city that the Sleepers saw, for there were no tall buildings. Evidently the centaurs' dwellings consisted of open space and large sheds. It was possible to get out of the weather, but there were no walls to enclose them.

"There is our leader," Moonwise called. Then he raised his voice. "Hail, Aramore. We bear a party from Goél."

Aramore's body was pure white. His hair was white to match. He had sky-blue eyes, and there were enormous dignity and power in his face. His voice was deep as he said, "Welcome to the Land of the Centaurs." Then his eyes searched the new arrivals. "I see you are tired from your journey. We must care for our visitors." He called out, and several female centaurs came forward.

"These will see to your comfort. Afterward we will have a council."

What followed was rather amazing. The Sleepers, Glori, and Beorn all slid to the ground, and the mare centaurs took them to one of the sheds. There a table was set, and one of their hostesses, a delicate-looking mare with the beautifully formed upper body of a woman, said, "We have plenty. You will eat, and then you must rest."

The banquet that followed was different—very different! The food was placed on tables almost as high as their heads. Evidently centaurs ate standing up. That may have been handy for them, but it was hard for the Sleepers and especially for Beorn. His head barely reached the top of the table.

Finally he grunted, "This is no way for a dwarf to eat." With a sudden motion he swung himself up onto the tabletop and sat cross-legged. "Now," he said grimly, "we can have our meal."

This brought a laugh from the others. It was the first time that any of them had laughed since losing Wash.

The food turned out to be delicious, consisting of vegetables and fruits. There was no meat on the table, and Dave said, "I guess centaurs are vegetarians." He looked at some centaurs trotting by and added, "They must have to eat a lot. Enough for a horse *and* a man."

They were later to find out that this was indeed true. The normal centaur banquet took several hours, for they ate slowly, chewing thoroughly, and as much as half of their day was spent just eating.

After the meal, Aramore himself came by. "I have come to look at your wounds, and then you will rest."

"I did the best I could, Chief Aramore," Abbey said, "but some of the injuries are old and haven't healed properly."

Aramore first looked at Sarah's swollen leg. He barked a command, and soon one of the female centaurs brought some leaves that had been steeped in boiling water. Aramore bound the leaves over the raw cut and said, "Now, my daughter, smell the fragrance of these."

Sarah put her nose over the steaming pot and breathed deeply. The smell was delightful, something like peppermint, and it seemed to go farther than her lungs. It spread throughout her body, filling her with a delightful sensation of rest and ease.

"I want you to rest, and this will make you sleepy. You all have pushed yourselves hard."

Aramore went around and treated every wound. But when he got to the dwarf, Beorn shook his head, saying, "There's nothing wrong with me."

"You are a stubborn dwarf—but then all dwarfs are stubborn. Open your coat."

Beorn tried to stare the centaur down, but that was difficult since Aramore towered high over him. Muttering, he pulled his shirt open and submitted to the ministrations of the centaur, who treated his wounds with a cooling salve. "This stitching was well done."

"Aye, it was that. The girl knows her business," Beorn said.

"All of you sleep now. When you have rested, we will talk."

"That was the best sleep I ever had," Sarah said, stretching luxuriously. She had been awakened by a female centaur, and she and Abbey had risen to see that they had almost slept the clock around. She stretched again and yawned. "I feel so refreshed."

"So do I," Abbey said. "There must have been something in that stuff we smelled that made us sleep." She ran her hand through her hair and said, "But I wish we could take a bath."

"Indeed you shall," a lady centaur said with a smile. She had a beautiful face with mild brown eyes. "Come, we will see to your needs."

She led them to a beautiful clear stream, and an hour later both girls were bathed and dressed and their hair had been arranged by another of the mare centaurs. Sarah felt like a new person as they approached the banquet shed.

"She's as good as any hairdresser I ever went to," Abbey said, patting the plaits that formed her corona of blonde hair. "I wish she could do my nails."

"I think they've done enough. But, look!" Sarah said suddenly. "The boys are already there—and our guides. It looks like another feast."

"Welcome to my table," Aramore said as the girls entered. "We will eat, and then we will talk."

It was another long meal, and the humans were filled long before the centaurs. However, it was only polite to wait, and during this time they learned a great deal about centaur habits.

Then Aramore asked, "Who is your leader?"

The Sleepers sat in silence.

It was finally Dave who said slowly, "Our leader, Joshua, has been captured—so until Goél appoints one of us, you can speak to me. I am the oldest but not necessarily the wisest."

"A good answer, David," Aramore said. "Tell us then why you have come."

Dave gave the essence of Goél's message. He concluded by saying, "Goél has asked that you and your people join with him in the final battle against the Dark Lord. All the free peoples of the world, all the House of Goél, will meet at the Plains of Dothan."

Aramore listened carefully and for a while appeared to be thinking deeply on the matter. He called a short recess during which he met with Moonwise and several other centaurs, evidently the leaders. Finally he came back and said clearly, "We will go to the Plains of Dothan at the command of Goél."

"That's wonderful, Aramore," Sarah said. "It makes the journey worthwhile—" But then she thought of Josh and Wash, and sorrow swept over her again. She lowered her eyes and said no more.

For some time the council made plans. When they concluded, Aramore said, "I will speak with you alone —the five Sleepers who remain."

Somewhat surprised, the Sleepers left the banquet hall and walked out into the open air. It was almost dark now, and the stars already twinkled brightly.

Aramore said, "We have heard of the prophecy of the Seven Sleepers. Now there are only five—and perhaps there will be even fewer."

Sarah held her chin high. "Josh and Wash both knew—we all knew—that serving Goél could bring death. We are not afraid."

Aramore considered her for a long moment, then

said, "I am convinced that the end of Nuworld as we know it is near. I have studied the prophecies. I have watched men and times. The world cannot go on as it is. Either Goél will rule with the free peoples, or we will all become slaves of the Dark Lord. It will be a hard battle, but my people and I are committed to Goél and to his House."

"Do you think we will win, Aramore?" Jake asked earnestly.

"Time will reveal what will come, but in the meanwhile I am disturbed."

"Disturbed? About what?" Dave asked with surprise.

"Something about your company is not right."

"Of course, it's not right," Reb said with some irritation. "We've lost two of our number."

"It is more than that. There is something in the spirit of your party that troubles me." Aramore's eyes grew half hooded. "Be very careful as you leave this place. You are going to the Land of the Magicians."

"That was the command of Goél." Dave nodded.

"A very unusual place—and a very unusual people."

"What's unusual about them?" Abbey asked quickly.

"They are powerful people. Not physically but in other ways. They have delved into the human mind, and they know how to sway the minds of others."

"But they're on Goél's side, aren't they?"

"Some are. Some are not. I have heard rumors that the Dark Lord has made inroads into Celethorn. I warn you again, be very cautious. It is a far distance, but I will send seven of my most trusted centaurs with you. They will bear you to the borders of Celethorn, then they must return to join the battle at the Plains of Dothan."

Early the next morning the five Sleepers and their two guides prepared to set out again. Glori listened closely as Aramore warned her of some dangerous country that lay ahead.

"My men will take you through, but there's always danger from the Dark Lord's servants. Be wary as you go to this place."

"Thank you, Aramore." Glori saluted him by bowing deeply. "We will long remember the centaurs."

"Goél be with you," Aramore said, and then he nodded toward the seven stalwarts that were led by none other than Moonwise. "Bear them safely. I feel somehow that the future of Nuworld itself is tied up with their well-being."

"Trust me, sire," Moonwise said. He galloped up to Sarah and smiled, "Are you ready, my lady?"

"Yes, Moonwise." Sarah raised her arms and was lifted to the centaur's back.

When all were in position, Moonwise held up an arm and made a gesture forward. "To Celethorn, the Land of the Magicians!"

8

Beorn Faces Death

This is sure a better way to travel than anything we've had lately!"

Reb was riding easily astride a centaur, enjoying its smooth gait as they passed over a small rise. The centaur, who said his name was Bendi, said courteously, "I'm glad you're enjoying our journey. What is the life of horses like back in your world?"

"Why, back where I come from, horses are real important. I learned to ride almost before I learned to walk. I was pretty much of a rodeo star too. High school rodeo, of course."

"Rodeo?" Bendi asked. "What is rodeo?"

"A rodeo? Don't you know what that is?"

"No, I think we do not have such things."

"It's where you let loose wild horses and fellas like me try to stay on for ten seconds before they get bucked off."

"Do the horses like . . . 'bucking'?"

"I don't guess they have much say about it. You see, they belong to the men who use them for rodeos."

"I would not like that." Bendi shook his head. "If I could not be free, I would rather die."

"Guess I'd feel the same way about it. But horses, they're—they're not like . . ."

"Not like us?" Bendi smiled. "How are they not like us?"

"Well, they're like the cattle you folks have. They

don't have minds like people, but they sure are nice. Some of them."

"Tell me about this bucking."

"Well, we put saddles on the bucking horses, then we get on, and the horse does all he can to throw us off, and we do all we can to stay on."

"They must not be very strong if they couldn't throw a little thing like you off in ten seconds."

Reb's pride was touched. "You don't know what you're talking about, Bendi!" he said. "Never was a hoss couldn't be rode."

Bendi lifted his voice and spoke to the other centaurs. "Listen to this human. He thinks he can stay on my back even if I wanted to throw him off."

Laughter went up.

Bendi said, "I would be a champion bucker back in your world. No human could stay on *my* back for ten seconds."

"That's what you think," Reb said. "You want to try it?"

Moonwise pulled up beside them just then. He said, "This is a good place for a camp. We will sleep here tonight and continue in the morning."

Bendi said, "My small human thinks he wants to try to stay on my back for ten seconds while I try to throw him off. With your permission, Moonwise?"

Moonwise stared at the young Southerner, who glared back defiantly. "I do not think it would be a good idea. You might break your neck, Reb."

"I don't intend to be tossed off. Just give me something to hang onto, and I'll show you."

"Hang onto my belt."

Indeed, Bendi did wear around his waist a belt with a knife stuck in it.

Reb took hold of the belt with his right hand. He

pulled his Stetson down firmly over his brow and said, "I'm ready. Let her buck."

Instantly Bendi rose into the air and twisted. It was a mighty twist, and it sent Reb flying through the air like an arrow shot from a bow. He turned a complete somersault and landed on his back. The air was driven from his lungs with a *whoosh*, and he got up slowly, complaining, "I wasn't ready. Give me another chance."

"Be careful. As I said, you might break your neck," Moonwise warned.

"Not me." He went back to the centaur and with one leap was on his back. Grasping the belt again, he pulled his hat down. "All right," he said, gritting his teeth. "Let her go."

Bendi began to buck, but this time Reb was prepared. He was tossed and thrown, and he almost slipped off, but somehow he managed to cling to the centaur's broad back. Loud calls sounded from the other centaurs, and Reb heard his friends whooping, "Ride 'im, cowboy!"

Suddenly Bendi stopped bucking and stood still. He turned and said in a kindly fashion, "You are a fine rider. I didn't think anyone could have done that."

Reb had been snapped and popped and jolted so fiercely that his vision was blurred. "Well," he admitted, "you're a pretty good bucker too. Don't know as I ever sat on a better one."

"Come now," Moonwise said. "We will eat and then rest—if the foolishness is over."

Later, after they had eaten and the centaurs were all bedded down, the Sleepers and their guides held a council.

"I'm glad the centaurs brought us this far," Dave

said. "It would have been a hard journey on foot. I wonder how much farther it is?"

"Not more than a day's journey," Glori said. "Over in that direction. It's dark, and you can't see now, but I know this country well."

"What sort of people are these magicians, Glori?" Jake asked. "Somehow I just don't like the sound of that. When I think of a magician, I think of a fellow doing card tricks."

"I do not know what a card trick is," Glori said, "but the magicians are very powerful."

"*Strong*, you mean, like the centaurs?" Dave inquired.

"No, not physically strong but able to do strange things."

"What kind of strange things? Tell us more about them," Abbey urged.

"For example, I have seen one of them pick up a stone that weighed over five hundred pounds—and without touching it."

"How could he do that?" Reb demanded. "That's impossible!"

"They do many things that seem to be impossible. I do not know how they do it, but we must be very careful. They are a rather eccentric group."

"What does *eccentric* mean?" Reb asked.

"It means crazy," Jake said. "Not like everybody else."

"Oh, I didn't understand that." Reb nodded. "I sure hope they don't decide to turn us into cats or something."

"I do not think they will do that," Beorn said. As usual, he sat outside the circle and was grasping his knees with his arms. "They are faithful to Goél—I should say at least *most* of them are."

86

Instantly Sarah asked, "What do you mean, 'most of them'?"

"I suppose in every land we go to, some will have been taken in by the wiles of the Dark Lord," Beorn said.

"I do not think that is so," Glori said. "I think the magicians are *all* faithful servants of Goél. You're always finding fault with everything, Beorn."

The dwarf did not answer her but gazed steadily across at the Sleepers.

For a while silence fell, and then Sarah said, "I miss Josh and Wash so much."

"So do we all," Dave said. "It's just not the same with them gone."

At midafternoon the next day, Moonwise held up his hand, and the column stopped. He turned to Sarah and lifted her to the ground. "We must leave you here, lady," he said. "I wish we could go all the way in, but those were the orders of Aramore."

"I know. Thank you so much." Sarah reached up and took the centaur's huge, muscular hands. "We couldn't have come this far without you."

The farewells were made quickly. Then Moonwise raised his head and looked toward the city that lay ahead of the Sleepers. "Be careful. Be very wary. We will see you at the final battle. Afterward, come back to our country sometime."

The Sleepers watched as the centaurs disappeared.

When they were out of sight, Dave shrugged uncomfortably. "It sure was a comfort to have them around. I don't mean just the ride, but they seem so wise and strong."

"They *are* wise and strong," Abbey said simply. "I wish they could stay with us all the way back to the Plains of Dothan. But I'm glad they're coming to the battle."

"I wish they could come with us to the city of the magicians," Jake said. "But I guess we have to get along without them."

"Let us start," Glori said. "We will go as far as we can today, but I think it will be tomorrow before we reach the city on foot."

After they had traveled for some time, Beorn said, "I will go ahead. It's wise to have a scout." Without asking permission of anyone, he slipped away.

Glori said, "I do not like that."

"What's wrong?" Dave said with some surprise.

"I do not trust Beorn."

"I do," Abbey said forcefully. "He's been faithful all the way."

Glori frowned. "I do not know why I feel this way, but I feel somehow that trouble lies ahead."

Beorn rejoined the group before evening however. "All seems clear ahead," he said. "I guess we're all right."

"We'll camp here tonight," Glori said. "Then we can make it easily into Celethorn tomorrow."

They set up camp. Fortunately there was fresh water nearby. Reb went hunting and came back soon with a small antelope that he had managed to shoot.

"Fresh meat," he announced. "Nothing like Mc-Antelope, is there? It's like a McDonald's back in the old days."

"I wish—" Sarah started to say, but suddenly a wild cry sounded from the growing darkness.

"Ambush!" Glori screamed. "Quick, this way!"

It appeared the Sleepers were nearly surrounded. They stumbled away from the ambush as best they could.

Then Abbey heard Dave cry out, and she said, "Are you all right, Dave?"

"Got me with an arrow! Right here in the arm . . ."

"Hurry," Glori said. "I think we can lose them!"

They floundered on through the deepening darkness. By the time they got clear, all were panting.

"Let me see that wound," Abbey said to Dave.

"It feels like it's on fire," he said when she had removed the dart.

"I think there was probably some kind of poison on the arrow," Abbey said. "We've got to go back to camp and get that leaf antiseptic."

"We can't go back," Glori said. "We'd all be captured." Suddenly she whirled and faced Beorn. "You're a traitor, Beorn." Beorn stood silently staring at the woman.

"You left us, and you knew the enemies of the Dark Lord were out there. I recognized their battle cry," she said. "You gave us away."

"That is not true," Beorn said.

"Where *did* you go, Beorn?" Jake demanded. "You would have seen those soldiers . . ."

"I saw no one."

"He is a traitor," Glori said, "and he must die!"

"Wait, wait! We can't kill anybody!" Abbey said. She went to Beorn and looked down into his face. "Did you betray us, Beorn?"

Beorn refused to answer. He stood silent, waiting.

Sarah said, "We can't execute anyone. Only Goél can give that command."

Glori scowled. "He will betray us again. I think he's done it before. How many times have we run into ambushes and traps—and always he's been the one out in front! I say execute him now." She slipped an arrow from her quiver and nocked it expertly, then drew the bow to full pull, with the arrow tip aimed at the dwarf.

Abbey leaped forward and pushed the bow aside. The arrow was knocked out of its path. It hissed through the air, passing not a foot from Beorn's body.

"There's no proof," Abbey said, facing Glori.

Glori said, "I am your leader. That was the command of Goél."

"No, you were just a guide, and you have guided us to the city. Your job is done."

Abbey was usually soft-spoken, but there was fire in her eyes now, and she put her hands on her hips. "If you want to do something helpful, go back and see if you can find that antiseptic."

"Say," Jake said. "I'd forgotten, but I believe some of the centaurs' special leaves got put in my pack." He pulled off his backpack and found the small packet of leaves. "Make a fire," he said. "We'll make a poultice out of these. It'll draw out that poison."

There was a bustle of activity, and soon Dave was feeling the coolness of the medicine on his arm. "That feels good," he whispered. He had grown very pale, and sweat had broken out on his face.

"Breathe some of the fumes too," Abbey said, helping him to sit up.

Dave inhaled deeply of the fragrant leaves. "That's good," he whispered, then seemed to drop off to sleep.

"He'll be all right soon. Maybe tomorrow," Jake said hopefully.

But Glori was frowning. "I tell you that dwarf will lead us all to our destruction!" That she was furious at being set aside was obvious. "Goél will not be pleased that you have allowed yourselves to be deceived by a traitor." Swiftly she walked several yards away and stood with her back to the group.

"I'm sorry, Glori," Abbey called after her, "but we can't take a life just because you're suspicious." Then she began stroking Dave's hair. "You'll be all right, Dave," she whispered. "You've got to be all right!"

9

Sarah Has Doubts

The Sleepers quickly discovered they had made another mistake. They were much farther from the city of Celethorn than they had thought. Glori determined this the next day after going on a scouting expedition. She came back with a worried expression on her face. "I was wrong. It is the ridge beyond the one you see where the Land of the Magicians lies."

Abbey was sitting beside Dave, who was lying flat on his back. He was still pale, and he had not recovered from the effect of the poison dart as fully as she had hoped. "Dave can't travel," Abbey said quietly. "He'll have to be a lot better than this before he can walk."

"We can't stay here," Glori said. She knelt beside him, putting a hand on his forehead. "I can see he's very ill. Why don't I go on ahead to Celethorn? I can make fast time, and when I get there I can return with a horse and wagon. The magicians can help him, I'm sure of that."

The Sleepers looked at each other.

Abbey said uncertainly, "That may be best. I don't think he'll be able to move for a few days." In her heart she was wondering if he would get well at all. He had been groggy, and his mind had wandered during the night.

"All right, then," Glori said. "You have a little food left. It shouldn't take me more than two days to get there, going as fast as I can—maybe less. And on the way back I'll have the horse and wagon. Say altogether three days at the most." She stripped off all her gear, saying, "I must travel lightly. Don't fear—I will bring back help."

The Sleepers stood watching as she loped lightly away, moving like a practiced runner.

Jake said hopefully, "Maybe she'll make it even quicker than she thinks." Then, looking down at Dave, he muttered, "He doesn't look good to me."

"He's not good," Abbey said, "and I don't know anything else to do for him."

Beorn said, "There are some herbs that my people use. I do not know if any grow around here, but I will look. They may help." He strode away.

Reb went off to collect firewood. He was still grieving over Wash.

Sarah sat beside Abbey and Jake. Her face was lined with despair, and she could hardly speak. "We're getting whittled down one by one. Josh, then Wash, and now Dave."

Jake patted her shoulder. "We just have to keep on. There's nothing else to do."

Reb managed to snare a rabbit, and they made stew. But by now it was growing dark. "I wish Beorn would come back," Jake muttered.

As if in answer to his wish, the dwarf emerged from the growing darkness. "I found the herbs!"

"Quick, give them to me," Abbey said eagerly. She listened as Beorn explained how they were prepared. Soon the pot was boiling, and the leaves were simmering. "These may be the same herbs the centaurs used," she said.

"Not the same," Beorn said, "but maybe they will help."

They treated Dave's wound by binding leaves over

the punctured flesh, which was now swollen, blue, and cold to the touch. Beorn raised Dave's head, and he inhaled some of the vapors, which seemed to revive him. He spoke feebly, "I'm a lot of trouble . . ."

"Don't say that." Abbey put an arm around his shoulders, saying, "Here—try to get some of this stew into you."

Dave ate a few bites, then shook his head. "No more." His voice was a mere whisper, and he lay back again on his bedroll.

Abbey sat beside him as the hours of the night passed. From time to time she would look out into the darkness and listen, but there was no sound.

Sarah made breakfast, and they ate although no one seemed hungry. Then they sat around idly waiting, for there was nothing to do. Not fifteen minutes later, Sarah jumped up. "There!" she cried. "Glori's coming—out of those trees."

"That's not Glori," Jake said. "Who else could be out here in this wilderness?"

"Guess we just have to see," Reb said. He loosened his sword from its sheath. "There's only one of him, but you never can tell."

The figure looked vaguely familiar to Sarah—something about the walk, the clothing. Then the newcomer lifted his head.

A thrill of unbelievable joy ran through Sarah. "*Josh!*" she cried and ran to meet him.

The others were right at her heels, and when they reached the lone figure, everyone babbled at once. "Josh, how did you get away? Are you hurt? How did you get here?"

"I'm all right," Josh said. "I'm all right." He looked well enough. His cheeks were a healthy color. "I wasn't all that badly wounded, and I managed to get away when the guard went to sleep."

Beorn came closer. "The guard went to *sleep?* That doesn't sound like the Dark Lord's guards!"

"What difference does it make?" Jake said impatiently. "Josh is here." He threw his arms around the boy. "Am I glad to see you! You must be hungry. How did you get here?"

"Did you come through the Caverns of Doom?" Beorn asked. His eyes were half shut, and he was studying Josh with a careful stare.

Josh faced the dwarf. "I've been in the city of the magicians. After I made my escape, I went there, and I learned many things. They know what is happening to all of us."

His speech, Sarah thought, seemed strangely stilted, somewhat mechanical and harsh. Her brow furrowed. "Josh, what's wrong? You don't sound like yourself."

"I've had a hard time," Josh said. And then he pointed at Beorn. "But *there* is the problem. That is who has brought all the terror into our lives."

Sarah stared at Josh in disbelief. "What are you saying?"

"The magicians have ways of knowing things. They say it was Beorn who betrayed us. He's responsible for Wash's death. He gave you away. He was responsible for my ambush too. All along he's been sending word to the servants of the Dark Lord." Josh suddenly drew his sword and started toward the dwarf.

"Wait!" Sarah stepped in front of him. "That's what Glori wanted to do. But—"

"She was right. She's been the true guide. There's the traitor!"

94

"But we can't kill a helpless man," Jake said. "If he is a traitor, we'll have to let Goél make that decision."

"He's responsible for Wash's death! Doesn't that make *you* want to kill him, Reb?"

Reb stared at Josh and then at Beorn. Slowly he said, "I don't know he's responsible, and I don't think you do either, Josh. These magicians, they're a little bit too slick for me."

"I'm the leader," Josh said. "That's what Goél said, isn't it?" Without waiting for an answer, he advanced again on Beorn, sword in hand.

Abruptly Beorn said, "Look at his chest."

"What did you say?" Sarah asked in bewilderment.

"Pull his shirt open and look at his chest. He has the smell of the Dark Lord about him—and if he is of the Dark Lord, he is not the Josh we knew. He'll have the mark of doom on his chest."

Josh let out a screech and threw himself at the dwarf. Sarah managed to push Josh so that the sword blade went wide. In one swift movement, Beorn knocked Josh down. At once he rolled him over and jerked the shirt aside.

"There, you see? The mark of the Dark Lord—the mark of doom."

"I don't understand. This is not Josh?"

"No," Beorn said. "The enemy has many such foul tricks as this. I've heard of this before. Somehow they can conjure up what looks like a real person, but he's not a real person. Look."

Before they could stop him, Beorn plunged his dagger into the throat of the form lying on the ground. Sarah screamed and then covered her eyes, for the figure suddenly shriveled up. It shrank and shrank until nothing was left but a little bit of black ash.

"It *wasn't* Josh," Sarah whispered. "I knew it wasn't Josh!"

"This proves one thing," Beorn said. "Somehow the Dark Lord knows where we are."

"Could one of the magicians in the city have done this?" Abbey asked. "If they can do a thing like this, we are not safe anywhere."

"We're not safe," Beorn agreed. "We must be on our guard. Anything we see must be tested. No one is to be trusted. No one."

The next day Dave awoke, his eyes clear. But his shoulder was painful, and he was not hungry. "Where are we?" he asked feebly.

"We're waiting for Glori to come back with a horse and wagon to take us into the city," Abbey said. "Here, you're spilling stew all over yourself. You must eat."

"What's happened since I've been unconscious?"

"For one thing, we saw a false Josh," Abbey said.

When Dave expressed astonishment, she told him the whole story.

He said slowly. "That's going to make things harder. We won't know a friend when we see one."

"Sure we will," Abbey said. "All we have to do is look at his chest. If they've got the mark of doom, they're the enemy."

"Did this Josh fool you?"

"Yes, he did, but I was so nervous and so ecstatic to see him, I guess it wasn't hard to fool me. He didn't fool Sarah, though."

"Well, she knows him better than anyone else. She's still grieving over him, of course. We all are."

"I haven't given up hope. I think Josh's still alive, and I somehow believe that we'll find him."

Dave took her hand. "You always believe good

things will happen, that the good people will always win." He held her hand lightly, then smiled. "I hope you always think like that."

Abbey flushed but did not pull her hand away. "I'm glad you're better, Dave," she whispered. "I was so worried about you. I couldn't stand it if anything happened to you."

His hand tightened on hers. She sat quietly beside him. They said nothing for long periods. It was a way they had come to have—to be comfortable with their silences.

On the third morning, Reb spotted someone approaching. "It looks like Glori coming, and she's got a wagon."

They all stood up to look. It was indeed Glori, riding a white horse. She was accompanied by a horse and wagon driven by a sturdy driver.

"How is Dave?" she called out.

"Much better," Abbey answered. "But I'm glad you brought the wagon. He really shouldn't walk."

"None of you will have to walk. Everyone get in. We're starting back at once for the city of the magicians."

As Abbey made a bed for Dave in the wagon, Reb asked, "What about these magicians? Did you meet any of them?"

"No," Glori said. "I was too anxious to get back here, but they know we're here. You can be sure of that."

"The Dark Lord knows we're here too," Beorn said grimly. "One of his emissaries found us last night. He came from that same direction." He pointed toward Celethorn.

She stared at him coldly and said, "Get in, dwarf, or walk if you please. I still think you're a traitor."

All were soon in the wagon. When Glori nodded, the driver spoke to the horses, and they moved ahead.

"I can't think Beorn is a traitor," Reb said softly to Jake. "Remember how he stood in the way of that polar bear? That was the act of a brave man. That was no coward's act."

"I know he's not a coward," Jake said. "That doesn't prove he's not a traitor. He could have done it to save his own hide."

"Do *you* think he's a traitor, Jake?" Reb asked directly.

Jake was a clever young man, smarter than most of the other Sleepers. He said nothing for a while. Then he said, "I think for sure we'll find out who's the traitor when we face Goél. No one could stand before *him.*"

10

Land of the Magicians

By the time Glori had led the wagonload of Sleepers deep into the plain toward Celethorn, Dave appeared to be worse again. He groaned every time the wagon hit a pothole. Indeed, all the Sleepers had their teeth jarred by the rough ride.

"We need to take it much slower," Beorn muttered. "Your friend is being shaken to pieces!" Beorn was sitting next to Abbey, who was supporting Dave in her arms to ease the ride as much as possible. The dwarf glanced at Glori; she was forging ahead at a rapid pace. "What good will it do to get to that blasted city of magicians quickly if the young man dies?"

"You're right, Beorn," Abbey said. "Tell the driver to slow down."

Beorn positioned himself behind the driver. "Slow down!" he commanded.

"I don't take my orders from no dwarf!" The driver was a bullnecked man with a beet-red face. He looked around and sneered. "Now, sit down, dwarfy, before I put you out to walk—"

He had no chance to say more. Quicker than thought, Beorn snatched a short, wicked-looking knife from his belt. Throwing his arm around the driver's throat, he pressed the tip of its razor edge into his backbone and said pleasantly, "I can drive a wagon better than you. If you don't slow down, I'll leave you to feed the buzzards."

"Wait . . . give a man . . . a chance . . . can't you?"

The driver was choking, for the dwarf's muscular arm was cutting off most of his air. When the arm gave a little, he gasped, "All right . . . slower it is."

"I knew you would be agreeable to suggestions." Beorn removed his arm but gave the knife a little push, bringing a yelp from the driver. "I don't want to have to bring this matter to your attention again," he remarked.

The driver brought the horses down to a slow walk, and Abbey flashed a smile at the dwarf. "Thank you, Beorn," she said. "This is much better."

"I don't expect her majesty up there will like it," Beorn prophesied.

He was exactly right, for Glori soon rode back, saying, "Why have you slowed down, driver?"

Beorn rose up once again and pulled his knife from his belt. "I requested he do so. He's shaking our injured man to pieces."

Glori glared at him, her eyes flashing. She was, indeed, a beautiful woman, but her beauty obviously made no impact on Beorn, who exchanged glares evenly with her.

"I see you're still creating all the trouble you can," she grated and clenched her teeth.

"It was necessary, Glori," Sarah spoke up. "Dave can't stand any more of that rough ride."

"Oh, I'm sorry—I didn't think. I was so anxious to get some medical aid for him . . ." Glori did appear repentant. She said, "We'll be there soon, even at this slow pace. I'll ride ahead and make sure things are ready. You can see the city from here." She pointed toward a smudge that broke the flat horizon—evidently the city of Celethorn.

As soon as Glori had ridden away, Beorn said sourly, "I wish that blasted woman would get lost!"

"You two really don't get along, do you, Beorn? Are you a woman hater?" Jake asked.

"I don't trust her."

"Well, she doesn't trust you." Jake shrugged. "I guess that's the way it is. Some people just don't get along together."

"My Uncle Seedy and his wife, Mamie, they didn't get along together," Reb remarked. "Stayed married for sixty years. Never had a pleasant day in their whole marriage."

"Why did they stay married?" Jake asked.

Reb stared at him in disbelief. "Why, they stayed married because they *was* married! You Yankees ain't got no idea of what marriage is really like. When a man gets married, he's got the woman that will have to do him as long as they live. Didn't you know that?"

Abbey smiled. "I like that idea, Reb." She wiped the perspiration from Dave's brow and studied his face. "I think that's the way it ought to be. One man and one woman, married as long as they live."

"That's the way it was done in Gum Springs, Arkansas."

"Gum Springs, Arkansas. That doesn't sound like a very big town," Jake said. "I don't remember that in my geography lessons. Where is Gum Springs?"

"Why, it's only two miles from Wet Wash—down next to Two Egg," Reb explained.

"Oh." Jake nodded. "I should have known that, of course."

Beorn listened in silence to all of this. The wagon rolled on. The driver, from time to time, cast a venomous glance at the dwarf, who stared back at him with a pleasant smile.

When they drew close enough to see the outlines

of Celethorn, Sarah stood up in the wagon and marveled at it. "That's some city!" she said with wonder. "Look at it!"

The wagon moved into the outskirts, and all the Sleepers expressed amazement. They were so used to rough villages built of whatever material was at hand—mostly logs or mud, and thatch for a roof—that Celethorn struck their eyes as a marvel.

The buildings, Sarah saw, were all constructed of some smooth material that she could not identify. They did not appear to be painted, and yet she could not discern a seam anywhere. The structures rose from the ground in graceful towers with turrets on top. Many were large and had rounded domes that seemed to be made of glass. The sun caught these, and the reflection of its beams made the city sparkle like a fairyland.

The streets were paved with a smooth, hard material over which the wagon wheels passed without a bump. The fronts of the buildings were pierced with glass windows, but Sarah could not see in through them.

"I'll bet those are like two-way mirrors," Jake announced. "People inside can see out, but those of us outside can't see in. Pretty neat!"

They passed through a business district lined with the usual enterprises selling food and drink and clothing. There were also many signs advertising "spiritual doctors."

"Spiritual doctor? I wonder what *that* is," Abbey remarked. "But the people do wear pretty clothes, don't they?"

She was looking at some citizens who stood watching the wagon trundle along the street. Their garments appeared to be made of silk and were of the brightest colors imaginable—red, orange, purple, vivid green. The women wore tall, peaked hats, and the men rather flat, soft caps. All seemed to have long hair, and the men, young and old, had beards.

Sarah noticed that many wore huge rings of various colored stones. "They look like emeralds and rubies," she said, "but they couldn't be. They're too big."

All in all, they beheld a colorful scene as they passed into the city of Celethorn.

Jake said, "If they can fight as well as they can build cities, Goél can use them in this battle that's coming up—but they just don't look like fighters to me."

"No, they sure don't," Reb agreed. "They look like stage actors all dressed up in their pretty clothes and fancy jewelry." He looked about uncomfortably. "Besides, I don't feel right about this place."

"Nor do I," Beorn spoke up. He was watching with a suspicious eye the citizens who lined the streets. "There is a strange air about this place," he said. "I don't like it."

"What have you heard about Celethorn, Beorn?" Sarah asked him.

"Some good things and some bad. From what I understand, there's plenty of both here."

"You mean, beside Goél's people there's black magic too?"

The dwarf glowered at a tall man who wore a pointed hat with stars and moons and suns imprinted on it. "I don't know anything about magic," he growled. "But they do strange things here, and we'd better be on our guard."

"But if Goél wants people from here, they can't be bad," Abbey said quickly.

"As I say, we can expect good *and* bad in Celethorn."

"That's true of every place we've ever been." Jake shrugged his sturdy shoulders. "We'll just take the meat and spit out the bones."

"That's easy enough with meat and bones," Beorn said, "but people aren't meat and bones. Sometimes fair seems foul, and foul seems fair. You can't always tell a book by its cover."

"Nor a man by his appearance," Sarah said. "Think about that awful thing that pretended to be Josh."

"And there may be worse than that here," Beorn said. "So beware. Look," he interrupted himself, "I think we've arrived at the palace."

The palace was a white structure, so white that it glistened and almost hurt the eyes. It was crowned with seven turrets from which colorful banners fluttered. Sarah noticed again that there were strange symbols on the banners.

The wagon pulled to a stop where Glori stood with a small, silver-haired woman dressed in a simple white gown. As they climbed down, Sarah noted that the woman had a stern face but at the same time had a kind look in her eye.

"This is Deormi, the chief priestess of Celethorn," Glori said. "May I present the five Sleepers?" She gave their names, then added, "And a dwarf who has helped guide them."

Deormi was small boned and unimpressive appearing, though her silvery hair was beautiful. It was impossible to guess her age—she could have been anywhere between forty and eighty—and though she was frail in body, something in her countenance and in her cool gray eyes told Sarah that they were in the presence of a powerful woman indeed.

"We have heard of the loss of your companions," Deormi said quietly. "It is a blow to lose a loved one."

Her words went right to Sarah's heart, and tears came to her eyes. *She understands,* she thought. *She really understands. It's not just talk.* "Thank you, Your Majesty," she whispered.

"Not 'Your Majesty.' We have no queen here. We are ruled by a council. I am the chief priestess at the moment, but you will learn about our ways later. For now, you have one who is seriously wounded . . ."

"Yes, Deormi," Abbey said quickly. She was still sitting in the wagon, holding Dave's head. "Please, can you do something to help him?"

"I will do what I can. Bring him into my quarters," Deormi said.

At once four servants—they wore simple gray clothing and appeared to be of the working class—stepped forward and lifted Dave from the wagon as though he were a child.

The Sleepers followed Deormi into the palace. Inside were richly tiled floors and fine paintings on the walls, and everywhere there were cleanliness and elegance.

The room that the priestess led them into was simple, however. "Put him on the couch," she said, then pulled up a low stool and sat beside Dave. Staring down at his still, gray face, she smoothed back his hair.

The Sleepers did not so much as say a word, for there was something of authority in the manner of the little woman.

Deormi removed Dave's shirt then and examined the injured arm. It had turned an angry red with fingerlike swellings around the wounded area. Then she went to a cabinet across the room where she quickly and efficiently mixed two potions. She brought back both and set one on a low table. The other was a paste that gave off a pleasant scent. She cleansed the wound, put the ointment on it, then said, "We will leave the wound unbandaged and let the air get to it." Then she reached down and with surprising strength lifted Dave to a sitting position.

His eyes fluttered, and his lips moved slightly.

"Here, my friend. You must drink this." Deormi lifted the other mixture to his lips and forced the liquid between them.

Dave swallowed convulsively, and a shudder ran through his body.

"Do not be alarmed. This is very powerful medicine," Deormi said reassuringly. "He is past the stage for simple remedies." Carefully she laid the young man down again, and for what seemed a very long time she simply sat at his side.

Sarah was watching Dave closely. His breathing had been quick and erratic. He had been almost gasping part of the time, but now, she saw with amazement, his breathing was slow and measured. "He's asleep," she whispered, "and it's real sleep. He's not just unconscious."

"You have a quick eye, young woman." Deormi smiled slightly. "I may sit with him for some time. In the meanwhile, all of you are tired and stained with travel. My servants will take you to your quarters. After you have been refreshed and have eaten, I will meet you in the council room. I understand that Goél has sent you to us on urgent business."

"Indeed, Deormi, that is true," Sarah answered.

"It is well that we not tarry. Go then, and after you are refreshed we will meet again."

Deormi nodded her head slightly, and Sarah noticed that a file of servants had come in. Each seemed to know what Deormi wanted without her speaking. One of them, a young lady dressed in an orange robe with a golden belt, approached Sarah and said, "This way, Lady Sarah."

Startled at the title, Sarah rose and followed, feeling dirty and awkward in the servant's presence. As they left the room, she heard the others being named, and then the girl led her down a series of corridors.

They came at last to a door that somehow opened without being touched. As Sarah was puzzling over this, she stepped inside and saw a beautiful room. It was large and fitted with furniture covered with gaily colored silks that looked very inviting. The walls glowed with hidden lighting, and one entire wall was open to the outside world. They could look out over the beautiful city of Celethorn.

"My name is Reeta," the servant said. "I will help you. You are very tired."

Sarah had never been so competently cared for in her life! After a luxurious bath, she sat before a mirror as her hair was arranged in a marvelously intricate fashion.

"You've done it beautifully, Reeta!"

"I'm glad you like it." The servant smiled. "Now, let me assist you with your dressing."

Sarah stared with amazement at the beautiful green silk gown that Reeta had chosen for her. The servant fastened the waist with a golden belt and then attached two small, exquisite green stones to her earlobes.

Sarah said, "I've never been taken care of so well in my entire life. This dress is a perfect fit."

"You look very beautiful, Lady Sarah," Reeta said. "Now then, I imagine your companions are all bathed and dressed as well. It is time for the meal. Will you come with me?"

Again Sarah followed her, almost reluctant to leave the beautiful room. They ascended several flights of stairs, then walked down a hall. Reeta stopped beside a small door, which slid open.

"Step inside," Reeta said, and when Sarah did so, the door closed. The small compartment moved upward smoothly without a sound.

"Why, it's an elevator!"

"We call it a *lifter*. You have seen one before? Very few people have."

"Oh, yes. Back in Oldworld."

Reeta's eyes glowed with interest. "Yes, I would much like to hear about your previous life—but that will have to come later," she said as the car stopped and the door opened.

Sarah soon found herself in a banquet room. It was a circular chamber with a circular table, and she saw that the other Sleepers and the two guides were already present. Deormi was there as well, seated beside a man who was tall and dark of hair and with swarthy features. His full black beard hid his mouth, and the turban on his head came down low on his brow. He wore a full-length gown with strange emblems impressed on it, and his eyes burned as they looked upon Sarah.

"Ah, the last of our guests is ready." Deormi smiled. "Sarah, this is Yanto, the chief magician of Celethorn."

"You're welcome, Sarah, to our city," Yanto said. "May I suggest we eat now, so that we can talk of the thing to be done?"

Sarah sat between Abbey and Jake. The food they ate at that banquet she would never forget. There was crisp salad of lettuce, carrots, radishes, and other delicious leafy vegetables that defied all her experience. This was followed by fresh, flaky fish that broke into delicious chunks as it fell from the bones. Then there was a roast, cut into tiny bits that they dipped into a delicious sauce. Finally there was what passed for ice cream but was smoother, colder, sweeter, and in flavors Sarah had never dreamed of.

When they had finished eating, Reb said, "I been to three county fairs and two snake stompin's—but I never had a meal like that in my whole life! Why, it's better than Aunt Jenny's barbecue!"

Deormi found his words amusing. "We appreciate your praise, Reb. I trust that all of you have enjoyed your meal. And now we will hear of your journey. Some of it we know, but do not spare the details. Sarah, perhaps you would be the speaker in this case."

Sarah flushed, for she was accustomed to either Josh or Dave doing the speaking. Nevertheless, as best she could, she began to tell how Goél had counseled them at the Plains of Dothan. She related that they had been sent to alert the tribes in the Land of Ice, the Land of the Centaurs, and the Land of the Magicians. She ended by saying, "It is the desire of Goél that you come and help him in the last battle."

As she spoke, she thought she saw a shadow pass over the face of Yanto. Now he glanced at the priestess and said quickly, "This is a matter for the entire council."

"Of course, Yanto. We will meet tonight. I will see that you guests are entertained," she told the Sleepers, "and when the council meets we will decide what must be done."

When the Sleepers were alone, Jake said, "It's not in the bag."

"What do you mean?" Abbey asked.

"I could see that they hadn't decided what to do," Jake said. "They may go to the Plains of Dothan, or they may not go."

The dwarf said, "I fear that they will *not* go. They

are too comfortable here. They know no fear and have not been touched by the Dark Lord—at least not outwardly."

"What do you mean, 'outwardly'?" Sarah asked.

Beorn would say no more, but his comment disturbed her. "I have confidence in Deormi," she said defiantly. "She's a good woman—I could tell that."

"Maybe so," Reb said doubtfully, "but that dude that was with her, he's got a hard look on him. I've seen his kind before. He's gonna give us trouble." He shook his head dolefully. "Why does there have to be one like that everywhere we go?"

11
The Sign

Sarah filed nervously into the council room with the other Sleepers, Glori, and the dwarf. The Sleepers seated themselves at one side of the chamber. Glori and Beorn stood behind them. She knew all were anxious to hear the council's decision.

They had left Dave behind. He had improved so much, even in a brief time, that he was sitting up and eating hungrily. He had even protested that he was able to go to this meeting, but Abbey insisted that he not push himself.

The council of Celethorn, Sarah saw, was composed of twelve priests. They sat about a table, a mixture of men and women, young and old, of vastly differing physical appearance. Deormi, the high priestess, sat beside Yanto. Their two chairs were slightly higher than the others, the only sign that they were in positions of authority.

Sarah thought that Deormi's face looked somewhat strained. She whispered to Abbey, "I wish this were all up to Deormi. I know she's on our side."

"I think she is," Abbey whispered back, "but I don't like the look on Yanto's face."

Deormi began to speak. "Once again I welcome the Sleepers to the city of Celethorn. We have heard of your fame and of your achievements and honor you for them. The council has been considering your urgent proposal, and we find ourselves in a deadlock." She glanced quickly at Yanto, hesitated, then said, "Some

111

among us are not certain that it would be wise for our people to join Goél in a war at this time."

"High priestess, may I speak?"

"Certainly, Yanto."

Yanto rose slowly to his feet and held the Sleepers steadily in his gaze. His face was thin, and there was a fanatical look in his dark eyes. "You must understand that we are constantly pulled between many forces in Nuworld." His high-pitched voice carried throughout the room. "Our knowledge and our scientific achievements, not to mention our psychic advances, have brought many from everywhere to ask for our assistance. Naturally, we must weigh all of these requests, for though our strength is great, it is not without limits . . ."

As Yanto rambled on, Sarah saw Reb lean across and speak to Jake.

"He's winding himself up to bust us—I can tell the signs."

"I agree with you, Reb. I don't like his looks."

"Back in Arkansas we had a politician that looked like him. He finally wound up stealing all the money in the county treasury and running off to Hawaii." Reb shook his head. "I don't like his looks, either."

Yanto finally completed his statement, and his eyes closed almost into slits. His mouth, too, drew itself into a fine line so that he looked hard and evil. "The council has voted, and I may tell you that the vote was deadlocked at six to six. It is unlikely that either side will change its viewpoint unless we have more information about the need to join in this war that is to come."

Deormi spoke up. "Do any of you care to answer Yanto?"

No one moved for a time, then Jake stood. He

made a pugnacious-looking figure, his feet firmly planted and spread apart, his hands on his hips. "Yes!" he said loudly. "I've got something to say."

Deormi seemed amused by the young man's audacity. "Speak on, then, Jake."

"OK, here's what I've got to say. Sometimes there's a lot of choices a fellow can make—maybe four or five of them. When you've got a situation like that, it's pretty tough. You have to weigh them all and try to sort out which ones are the most important and finally narrow it down to one." He fixed his eyes on Yanto and said, "But *this* time there are only two choices."

"And those two choices are . . ." Yanto demanded.

"Either we serve Goél and the free peoples of the world, or we fall in with the Dark Lord—and you all know what that means, I hope."

Yanto glared. "You are a *child!*" he exclaimed. "You know nothing of high matters. We speak here of the destiny of Nuworld itself, and children must not be allowed to make decisions of that magnitude."

"But Goél seems to trust the decisions of these . . . children, as you call them, Yanto," Deormi said mildly.

"We do not know *what* Goél is doing. Where is he? Why isn't he here? If he wants us to fight his wars, he should come himself."

Jake protested. "Goél can't be *everywhere.*"

Yanto spat out, "And since he is not here, it is up to this council to decide what will be our decision."

"What do we have to do to convince you?" Jake asked.

Yanto's face underwent a change. He lost his angry look, and his voice grew milder. "That is well spoken, my young friend. What must you do to persuade us? This is a large question indeed! You are asking us to risk our lives, our city, indeed our very destiny. It would take a great thing to convince us that this is the course that we should follow."

Jake seemed somewhat suspicious at the smooth tone of the priest. "I'm no orator," he said. "People either believe in Goél, or they don't."

"Ah, but that is not quite true. There are some who are honestly in doubt," Yanto insisted. He looked over the council, half steadfast in their decision to follow Goél, half equally determined not to. "You cannot ask us to risk all that we have without some proof that Goél should be followed."   .

"What sort of proof would you demand, Yanto?"

The speaker was, unexpectedly, Glori. She had stepped forth from where she had been standing behind the chairs of the Sleepers, and there was a strange smile on her face. "Name your proof."

"You are an outspoken young woman, but I will answer you in like fashion," Yanto said. "We all know that the Dark Lord has mysterious and potent powers. It will not be swords alone that will defeat him, nor spears, nor arrows. The victor in this war will be those with the highest spiritual powers. Do you agree?"

Jake glanced quickly at Sarah, who nodded slightly, and at Reb, who shrugged. "Well, I guess that's right. So what?"

"Then I do not think it would be unreasonable if this council asked to see a sample of your powers."

A silence fell over the room, and Jake's face was a study in shock and amazement. Yanto's trap had closed on him. He swallowed once and then tried to speak, but so great was his surprise he could only say, "Why, you can't expect us—"

"Oh, but we can." Yanto nodded vigorously. "In our country even the very young learn the basics of magic.

114

Even ten- and twelve-year-olds learn to do minor bits of magic—such as causing a stone to rise in the air without being supported . . ."

"I'm no magician," Jake mumbled.

"Ah, that is very true," Yanto said slowly and with great emphasis, "but by saying so you are admitting that you have no spiritual power."

Sarah spoke up suddenly. "There's more to spiritual power than doing tricks!" she exclaimed. "We're not talking about pulling a rabbit out of a hat. Those things are illusions anyway."

"Do you think so?" Yanto said, and his thin lips turned upward in a smile. "I do not agree, nor do any of the council. For example, is *this* an illusion?"

To her shock and horror, Sarah felt herself rising out of the chair she was sitting in. She hung suspended two feet above it.

A gasp went around the other Sleepers. The council members showed sharp interest.

Yanto said, "Would you call this an illusion, my friends?"

"Put her down!" Reb growled.

"Certainly, my young friend."

Yanto nodded toward Sarah, who sank slowly back into her chair. She gave a gasp and grabbed the chair arms for support.

"A very minor sort of magic," Yanto said. "Not at all important, but I trust it proves my point." He looked toward the council members. "The Sleepers come asking us to risk all that we have, our very nation, and yet they themselves are powerless."

"They cannot be *utterly* powerless," Deormi said sturdily. "We have evidence of how they have overcome the Dark Lord time after time."

"Ah, yes, we have *reports* of such things," Yanto

said, "but no evidence. I think we must have more than that. We must have a sign."

Sarah's heart sank. She had heard of the powers of the Celethorn magicians, and this one sample convinced her that there was something to it. Yet she could not for the life of her think of any response to the argument that Yanto had given.

I've got to do something, she thought. *We can't let them defeat us.* Aloud she said, "Council of Celethorn, I cannot answer the matter that Yanto has put before us. It is true none of us has *magical* powers. It is true also that we are young and inexperienced, but one other thing is true. We have met Goél. Those of you who have met him know that, despite his common appearance, he is more than he appears. One day," she said firmly, "we will see the true power of Goél burst forth. When that happens, those who have opposed him will taste hard justice."

"Ah, our young friend is a prophetess." Yanto smiled cynically. "Prophets, however, come rather cheap in this part of the world. What we value is a *sign*."

The debate continued for a long time. The Sleepers argued desperately that the magicians must throw their powers on the side of Goél. Yanto skillfully fielded every plea and logically destroyed their evidence. There seemed nothing the Sleepers could do to change his mind or the minds of the negative council members.

At last Yanto said, "Perhaps by now some of the council have seen the helplessness of the Sleepers. I honor them for what they may have done in the past, but these are new days. New times demand different methods. Once again, I am going to ask for a vote, and I will not ask our young friends to leave the room. But before we take the vote"—his voice changed suddenly,

116

his eyes glittered, and he pulled at his beard with excitement—"I am going to offer them proof that they are following the wrong flag."

"What do you mean?" Sarah asked.

"I'm going to give you such evidence of the power of the magicians of Celethorn that you yourselves will agree to abide by *our* decision."

"You'll never make me agree to leave Goél," Sarah said, and the others murmured in assent.

"No? Then let me show you another small sign of my own, Sleepers."

Yanto clapped his hands and nodded at the two servants who stood as guards by the door. At his signal, they opened the door, and Yanto cried out with a piercing voice, "Enter the council room, my young friend!"

The Sleepers all stood to their feet and faced the door. The dwarf, Beorn, had said absolutely nothing thus far. He had been standing as far from Glori as he could get. Now he whirled with the others, his face dark with suspicion.

Sarah's eyes opened wide with shock as Josh Adams walked through the door! She opened her mouth to cry out but then thought instantly of the false Josh. *They won't fool me again*, she thought grimly. *If this is the work of the Dark Lord, I'll find out!*

Josh walked up to the Sleepers. He looked tired and pale, but his eyes were bright, and he was smiling. "Hello, Sarah," he said cheerfully. His eyes ran around the room, and he greeted the other Sleepers, then his brow furrowed. "Where're Wash and Dave?"

Sarah sought desperately to find something wrong in his voice. But this Josh sounded like the old Josh Adams she knew—though his eyes did seem somewhat brighter than she would have expected after a difficult time. She said carefully, without approaching him, "Josh, where have you been?"

Josh turned to her. "I was captured by the soldiers of the Dark Lord, but for some reason they turned me over to the magicians here in Celethorn. I was almost dead, and the magicians healed me." He moved his shoulder, saying, "I'm almost well now, though I've lost a little weight." Again he asked, "Where're Dave and Wash?"

"Wash is dead—and Dave's wounded," Sarah said bluntly.

"Dead! Oh, no!" Josh exclaimed. "Not Wash!"

His grief seemed so real that Sarah could not help going to him. "Is it really you, Josh?" she asked, her voice trembling.

Josh stared at her. "Is it really me? Of course, it's really me. Who else would it be?"

"Another Josh came to us before we came here. We all thought it was you at first, but it turned out that it was just an image made by some of the Dark Lord's powers."

"Look at his chest," Reb called out suddenly.

Josh looked over at Reb. "Look at my chest?" he asked in amazement. "Whatever for?"

"Because the false Josh had the mark of the Dark Lord on his chest," Sarah said. "Would you mind if I looked?"

Josh glared. "Don't you believe me, Sarah? You know me better than anybody."

Sarah wanted to say, "Yes, I do believe you," for desperately she wanted to know that Josh was alive and well. But experience had hardened her somewhat, and she said, "If you're the real Josh, you won't mind letting me see your chest."

A silence fell across the room. It seemed all the Sleepers held their breath.

Finally Josh nodded slowly. "I'm just sorry you don't trust me," he said stiffly. "Here, look." He unbuttoned his shirt and bared his chest, saying, "No sign of the Dark Lord, is there?"

"No!" Sarah cried and was filled with a rush of happiness. She looked at the others and said, "It's really Josh—back again." She wanted to throw her arms around him but was too embarrassed to do that.

Yanto said quickly, "Now, you see the power of our council and of our people. We have restored the lost Sleeper to you. Are you convinced now of our true powers?"

Sarah was confused. "I'm thankful Josh is back, of course . . ."

Yanto interrupted. "Josh, perhaps you would like to retake your place. You are the leader of the Seven, as I understand."

"I suppose it's only the Six Sleepers now," Josh said solemnly. He shook hands with each of his friends, then remained standing while the others sat. "I will speak for the Sleepers," he said, and his voice rang with authority. "What is being decided?"

Yanto said, "Your friends have asked us to go to war. I have asked them for a sign that this is the right thing to do, but they have given none. You have been with us magicians for some time. What is your feeling about joining Goél?"

Josh said confidently, "Goél did send us to summon you, but now he's appeared to me and commanded me to change our mission."

Sarah gasped. "Josh, what are you saying?"

Josh faced the Sleepers. "I've learned a lot since living with the magicians. They are wise, and they've shared their wisdom with me. And now I've had a visit from Goél, and we talked a long time. He wants the magicians to stay here and not join him at Dothan. We're to remain here too."

"That can't be!" Jake exclaimed.

"You'll have to take my word for it," Josh said. "You know what Goél is like. Sometimes he gives commands that seem strange. You remember that, Sarah, from our first adventure. He gave you a command and said nothing to the rest of us."

Sarah did remember how Goél had appeared to her and commanded her to trust him and obey. The others had not believed, and she had had the greatest struggle of her life obeying.

"I . . . I know that's true, Josh, but . . ."

"I'm afraid this time I'll have to assert myself as leader. We'll stay here with the magicians. There's much for all of us to learn here."

Sarah could not put her finger on it, but *something* was different about Josh. She recognized that the difference was not in his voice or in his appearance. He certainly was the same Josh physically, but there was a difference in the expression of his eyes and certainly in his manner.

Josh has always been so humble and meek—but now he's giving orders in an arrogant way, she thought.

Josh was indeed speaking confidently and with an air of great authority. "We must, of course, obey the voice of Goél."

"Of course, you must," Yanto agreed, "and since your leader has commanded you to stay here, the council welcomes you."

Deormi shifted uncomfortably in her seat, her wise eyes studying the Sleepers. She said, "This is your decision then, Sleepers, that we *not* join battle with Goél at the Plains of Dothan?"

"That's right," Josh said quickly. He turned to the others. "We all agree, don't we?"

Sarah saw that every Sleeper looked uncomfortable. They had thrown everything they had into this mission for Goél, and now their efforts seemed to have been for nothing.

"I don't like it, Josh," Reb said suddenly. The tall Southerner usually had little to say about command decisions, but now his light blue eyes were half closed, and he studied Josh thoughtfully. "I lost the best friend I ever had on this mission. Wash's death doesn't mean anything if we don't go through with it."

"We *are* going through with it!" Josh exclaimed. "Don't you see, Reb? Wash's life won't be lost. It's just that Goél has changed our orders. Now, instead of going back to Dothan, we stay here."

Reb shook his head stubbornly. He was not a quick thinker, but once he got an idea, he would carry it through if it killed him. He had no words to answer Josh, and he stood there saying nothing. But, clearly, something did not feel right to him.

Then Abbey spoke up. "Could we have time to talk about this among ourselves?"

"Why, certainly," Deormi said immediately. "We will declare a recess. You may go, and I trust that you will find Dave much better."

As the council members moved out through a back door, the Sleepers began to question Josh.

Sarah herself said little, but she kept watching his eyes.

When finally they started walking back to where Dave was resting, she followed along, still very quiet.

"You're not saying much," Abbey whispered.

"No, I don't feel right about this."

"Neither do I, Sarah," Abbey said quietly. "Goél

can change his tactics, I suppose, but to flip-flop his whole general plan like this doesn't seem like Goél. Besides, there's something . . . well . . . *different* about Josh. I don't like what these magicians have done to him."

Dave was sitting up when the other Sleepers entered his room, and his face had good color. He experienced the same shock and amazement as the others on seeing Josh. After Dave had greeted him, and Josh had told of his strange adventures, Dave said, "Well, then, everything's all right, isn't it?"

When silence fell over the room, Dave looked at the faces of the others. "What's the matter?" he asked. "Is something wrong?"

Josh said, "We've had a visit from Goél, Dave. The plans have been changed." He explained the situation and then said, "We haven't always agreed on things, but this time I'll just have to say that this is the way it will be." He smiled.

There was a hollowness in his smile that disturbed Sarah, but still she said nothing.

"Well, I have a meeting with some of the council," Josh said. "I'll bring back a report afterward."

After he had gone, Dave looked up at Sarah. "He's Josh, but he's . . . changed . . . hasn't he?" he asked quietly.

"Yes, he has." Sarah frowned. "I can't put my finger on it. It's Josh, all right. He's even got the little scar on his cheek that he got in the battle with the tigers. The exact scar in the exact place. It's his body all right, but . . ."

Gloom seemed to have fallen over the chamber. Sarah turned and went out.

Soon Abbey was left alone with Dave. She put her hand on his forehead, then smiled. "Your fever is all gone."

"I feel much better." He moved his arm. "They're wonderful with wounds here. Look—I couldn't even move that arm. Now, it's practically well. Just a twinge."

"Dave . . . I'm worried about what's going on."

"You mean about Josh and this new plan?"

"Yes. Sarah doesn't believe in it, and she doesn't trust Josh."

Dave whistled softly. "Well, if *Sarah* doesn't trust him, where does that leave the rest of us? They were always the closest of friends." He stood up and tested his weight. "I'd better get my strength back," he said. "It looks like we're going to have to make a pretty hard decision soon."

12

The Real Josh

Never had Sarah been so confused or disturbed than she was after the meeting with Josh.

Or *was* it Josh?

She went over the scene in her mind, trying to remember word for word what had been said. "It *has* to be Josh," she whispered as she walked up and down her room, wringing her hands. He had that scar on his face, and in every detail he was the same.

But what about the way he talks? The way he thinks?

Sarah threw herself down on a soft orchid-colored couch that comfortably adjusted itself to her body. Even something about *that* disturbed her. She did not *like* this Land of the Magicians. All of her needs were cared for; she was not hungry, or thirsty, tired, hot, or cold—still, something about the place troubled her.

"I'd feel better if we were out in a jungle with tigers or under the ocean trying to get away from sharks!" she exclaimed bitterly, leaping up from the couch. "Oh, Goél—Goél! Why don't you come to me? Tell me if what Josh says is right or not!" She waited, as if expecting Goél's voice to sound within her chamber, but nothing broke the silence.

In despair, Sarah left her room, walked down the hall, and made her way out of the palace. She walked the streets of Celethorn for a long time. As she moved among the citizens, she imagined she drew sharp glances. Was there something alien about her to these wizards? She stopped once and stooped to pet a hammerheaded yellow tomcat that wandered up to her and said, "Meow."

"Hello, Tom." She smiled. "I wish I had some fish to feed you. You'd like that, wouldn't you?" When the cat meowed again, she made up her mind. Picking up the huge tom in her arms, she started for a shop across the street.

"I'd like some fish, please."

"What kind of fish?"

"Any fish that cats like."

The clerk, a tall, thin man, stared at her uncomprehendingly. "You're going to feed my fish to that stray cat?"

"Yes, and put it on the bill of Deormi, high priestess of Celethorn. I am Sarah, one of her guests."

The clerk still stared at her, then forced a smile. "Certainly. I'll have it ready for you right away."

Five minutes later Sarah was outside, had opened the wrapping, and was feeding small chunks of fish to the cat. "You can have all you want," she whispered. "You're getting just what you asked for. I wish I could!"

When she had satisfied the cat and petted him once more, she returned to the palace. "No sense walking the streets," she muttered. When she entered the hallway on the floor where the Sleepers' rooms were located, she was accosted by Beorn, who suddenly appeared from around a corner.

"This way, Sarah," he said huskily.

"What is it, Beorn?"

"We've got to talk." The dwarf led her to a room half filled with supplies. "I don't want anybody to hear us," he said. His dark face was severe with strain. "I don't like what's going on, Sarah."

"I don't like it, either," she replied. "What do you think of Josh?"

"You know him better than anyone else, but he doesn't seem the same to me as when we started this journey."

"He *looks* the same," Sarah said.

"Looks can be deceiving. The false Josh that we turned to cinders looked like your friend. But this one *talks* different."

"I think he *is* different." Sarah had been thinking of little but Josh since their encounter, and now she said slowly, "Beorn, I believe these people are treacherous—I should say, *some* of them are."

"You suspect Deormi?"

"No, I suspect Yanto."

"So do I. What do you think he's done?"

"I think somehow he got Josh away from the ones who captured him, but then I think they've brainwashed him."

Beorn stared at her. "Brainwashed? You mean took his brain out and—"

"Oh, no, no, not *literally*," Sarah said quickly. "I mean . . . somehow they've put him under a spell." She was satisfied that Beorn would understand that. When his eyes at once narrowed, she said, "I see you've thought of that too."

"Yes, I have, but what are we going to do about it? It would be wrong to give up on these people." The stubborn dwarf clenched his knotty fists, looking as if he would like to strike someone. "You remember what Goél said—one sword could make a difference. These magicians are powerful. Some of them are evil, but that's the way it is with power."

"What do you mean, Beorn?"

"I mean that power can be used for either good or

for evil. The Dark Lord has power. He's used it for his own selfish desires—and used it cruelly. I think the council and the citizens here could be of great help in the battle that is to come if they would decide to use their powers for good."

"You're right, Beorn," Sarah said slowly. "But what are we to do?"

"That is beyond me. I am merely a guide. You are one of the Sleepers—and since Josh, your leader, is obviously unable to function, I think the rest of you will have to take action."

Immediately Sarah made up her mind. "Come along. We've got to have a meeting."

Sarah and Beorn summoned the other Sleepers at once, and soon the small group was gathered outside the palace gates. Sarah said, "I don't trust that place. They might have hidden microphones or something."

"Meeting outside is a smart idea," Jake said. "It's time we started showing some sense."

When the group reached a small grove of trees in a park some distance from the palace, Sarah said, "Beorn and I have been talking. I guess we're all wondering what to do."

Jake said, "What *can* we do, Sarah? Josh is the leader."

"But I don't think he's the *same* Josh," Sarah said.

"He didn't have the Dark Lord's mark on his chest," Abbey reminded her.

"I know that. It's Josh all right, but I think his *mind* is a prisoner somehow."

Dave was with them this time, not yet as strong as he had once been but glad to be out from under the pain of his wound. Taking a deep breath, he said, "From what I understand, he's not thinking or talking or acting like the old Josh. Josh would never be one to give up on a mission."

"But he says he's seen Goél," Reb said. "What about that?"

Silence fell over the group, and Sarah knew this was the crux of the whole problem. None of them would go against the orders of Goél.

With a burst of energy she said, "I once heard someone say that the eyes are the window to the soul. You know what that means. You can look into people's eyes sometimes and tell what's inside of them." She saw their nods. "Have any of you looked close into Josh's eyes?" When no one spoke, she said grimly, "Well, I have, and it's like—it's like looking into an empty room! Josh's eyes were always so warm, and he was so honest you could tell what he was thinking. Somehow there's a . . . well, a coldness in him now. And I think what we're seeing is not a false Josh but a Josh who's somehow been imprisoned in his mind."

"By george, I think you're right!" Jake exclaimed. "He's just not himself. He's bossy, he's throwing orders around, and that's just not like Josh."

"We've got to have a confrontation," Sarah said. "I've been thinking about it a lot. These magicians are powerful, and if Josh is in the power of the Dark Lord—if somehow Yanto's done that to him—there's no point in our trying to overpower them with physical force."

"Then what can we do?" Abbey asked helplessly.

"There's something we have that they don't," Sarah said slowly. "We have Goél, and we have love, and they don't. Somehow I think that love is stronger than hate," she said quietly. "And here's what we're going to do . . ."

At the next council meeting, satisfaction was glowing in the eyes of Yanto. He looked toward the Sleepers, who stood together in a group. He glanced past them to where the dwarf stood, arms folded, his face dark with displeasure. He glanced at Glori, who stood as far away from the dwarf as she could.

"We must make the final decision," Yanto said smoothly. "Josh, have you brought your friends around to understanding the real situation?"

Josh was clothed today in clinging blue silk. He looked out of place to Sarah, who was used to his old khakis and his careless dress. "Yes, I think we are all in agreement." Turning to the Sleepers, he said, "We agree to—"

"Just a minute!"

Sarah took a step forward. She looked at Josh and said, "Josh, come back from wherever you are." Her voice was loud and rang with authority.

Josh's mouth dropped open, and he stared at her blankly. Then his face grew taut. "Sarah, be quiet! I'm the leader and—"

"Josh—" She went to him and put a hand on his arm. He flinched, but she said softly, "We all love you, but you're not *here*. Wherever you are, Josh, come back to those who love you!"

Josh began to tremble. "Get away from me," he said harshly.

Sarah knew that all the Sleepers now had their eyes fixed on Josh, longing to see him brought back from wherever he was imprisoned.

"Think of all of our times together," she pleaded. "How we've suffered, yet we've rejoiced, Josh. We've come so far together. It's not just your body—it's your mind that we want. Come back, Josh—"

Josh drew himself up straight, his face pale. His

teeth were clenched, and his eyes were wide and frightened. "No—no," he cried. "I *am* Josh!"

But Sarah softly continued to plead. "We know you're Josh. But we want your *mind* free . . ." She did not show anger, nor did any of the other Sleepers.

She knew that the battle was, indeed, spiritual. She glanced over Josh's shoulder to see Yanto and three of his fellows hurling all their powers against them. Their eyes were burning, and the room had become a battleground where unseen adversaries threw themselves against the minds of the Sleepers. Sarah felt as battered in mind as she had ever felt in body throughout their entire adventures. Inwardly she cried out, *Goél—Goél, help me!*

She was aware that the other Sleepers were struggling as well. Dave, who was still weak from his wounding, slumped so that he almost fell. Reb and Jake stepped to his side and held him up, Reb murmuring, "Hang in there, Dave! We'll ride this hoss!"

Then Josh jerked his arm away from Sarah and said, "I don't need your love!"

Sarah looked into his wild eyes and remembered the gentle boy that she had known for so long. "Yes, you do need our love, Josh. Everyone needs love. The worst thing in the world is to be cut off from love."

Josh screamed and fell to his knees.

"Remember Goél, Josh!" Sarah cried. And then, lifting her voice, she cried out, "Oh, Goél, bring Josh back to us!"

"Obviously the leader has become ill," Yanto said quickly. "We will have him taken away so that we can treat him."

"Leave him alone!" Sarah's eyes flashed as she stepped between Josh and Yanto. Then she turned and knelt beside the boy. "Josh," she whispered, "we love you. We'll always love you no matter what happens. Come back to us, Josh!"

Suddenly Josh's body collapsed.

Sarah first thought in terror, *He's dead!*

But then his lips moved, and his eyes opened.

And instantly Sarah saw the change. "Josh, you're back!" she cried. She turned to the other Sleepers. "His mind is back! I can tell by his eyes. He's back."

All the Sleepers gave glad cries and rushed to him. Reb and Jake pulled him to his feet and looked into his face.

"You're right—it's the old Josh! Are you all right, boy?" Reb demanded.

Josh passed a hand over his face. He blinked and then shook his head as one who had been awakened from a terrible dream. And then a smile came to his lips. He said hoarsely, "It's good . . . to be back."

"Obviously the leader needs help," Yanto cried. "Take him to my chambers."

Two guards started for Josh, but one found himself almost impaled on the short knife that Beorn had drawn and aimed directly at his stomach. The other found his arm twisted behind his back by Reb Jackson.

"We can do without help from you, thanks," Sarah said. "Josh, do you know what's happened?"

Josh straightened up. "Yes . . ." His voice was still hoarse as if from disuse. He looked at Deormi and said, "I was put under a spell by some of your people, Deormi."

The priestess frowned. "It was not of my doing. What has happened?"

Josh suddenly pointed at Glori, "*She* delivered me into the hands of our enemies—and she told them to bring me to this place. Then she and that one—" he pointed to Yanto "—tried to turn me away from Goél."

"It's a lie," Glori called out, but her face had turned pale, and her voice was not steady. She looked at the chief magician. "We must do something, Yanto!"

"Shut your mouth, fool!"

But it was too late. Josh said, "She's a servant of the Dark Lord!"

"It's a lie!" Glori screamed again, but guilt was written on her face.

Sarah started toward the blonde woman. Before Glori could move, Sarah grabbed the fabric of Glori's garment and pulled. There was the sound of ripping cloth, and then a gasp went over the room. High on Glori's chest was the same mark that had been on the chest of the false Josh!

"She's in the service of the Dark Lord, all right!" Josh said.

Glori whipped a dagger from her belt. Quick as a striking snake she leaped toward him.

But the dagger never reached its target. The knife of Beorn, the dwarf, flashed, and the woman gave a wild cry and fell to the floor.

The high priest gave a signal.

"Watch out for Yanto!" Dave yelled.

"Take them prisoner!" Yanto cried.

Three council members stepped forward, then three more. They did not attack the Sleepers with knives or spears or swords but threw such terrible mental force against them that Sarah felt herself nearly paralyzed.

Josh seemed to be slipping away. He murmured, "After all this . . ."

"Don't give up, Josh," Sarah said, panting and struggling with the force of the magicians' power. "Goél will not let us perish."

Then a voice said, "In the name of Goél, *stop!*"

It was the priestess, Deormi. She spoke then in a language Sarah did not understand, and immediately her followers on the council surrounded Yanto and his henchmen.

Sarah watched the tremendous struggle between the powerful council members, but she soon saw that Deormi and her people were stronger. She could almost feel the force of Yanto and his men slipping away.

Suddenly Josh stood to his feet, seeming to have complete freedom once more. He reached out and hugged Sarah as Deormi gave commands and servants seized Yanto's arms.

"He cannot be bound with cords, but I will bind him," Deormi said firmly. She fixed her eyes on the chief magician, and after a brief struggle Yanto quieted. He made no objection as the guards led him and his three fellows out of the room.

Deormi turned to the Sleepers. "This has been a hard thing for us. It is never pleasant to find traitors in your midst."

"No, it is not pleasant." Beorn, the dwarf, looked down at the body of Glori. "This one was in a high place. She could have been great in the service of Goél, but after he assigned her to this mission she was somehow drawn away, and she chose the way of the Dark Lord."

Abbey looked at Glori and whispered, "I feel sorry for her. She would've destroyed us, but now she is destroyed."

Silence fell over the room, and then Josh said, "What will you and your people do, Deormi?"

The priestess drew herself up. She was not tall or strong physically, but there was power in her voice as she said, "We will lend our strength to the House of Goél!"

13
Old Friends

The Plains of Dothan, for as many years as men could remember, had been a field, flat as a table, used by wild sheep and cattle. The mountains that ringed it formed a kind of huge amphitheater.

Dave Cooper shoved back his steel battle helmet to clear his vision and said, "Abbey, this reminds me a little bit of playing football for the Cowboys. Those mountains are like the stadium seats, and the plain is about as level as a football field."

Abbey was wearing a steel breastplate that was somewhat too large. It caught the sun overhead and flashed like silver. Now she, too, glanced at the distant mountains, covered with blue haze. Then she looked at the host gathered for battle and said quietly, "I think this is a little more serious than football."

Dave's eyes swept the battle line composed of the followers of Goél, and his countenance grew tense. "You're right about that." He unsheathed his sword, tested it with a finger, and studied it carefully. He had stayed up most of the night sharpening his weapons, as had the other Sleepers. Presumably so had the other warriors who were assembled to stand against the Dark Lord. Now he looked into the distance and narrowed his eyes. "They're coming," he said softly. "We'd better be ready. I think it's going to be pretty bad."

The Sleepers had returned to Dothan accompanied by Beorn and Deormi's small army, and Goél greeted them at once. Dave still remembered the relief

135

he felt upon seeing their leader again. Goél was very busy with the captains of the various segments of his army, but he found time to commend each Sleeper and also to warn them that the battle ahead would be more fierce than anything they had yet seen in their service for him.

Now, for several days, scouts had come back, all reporting the same thing: a mighty host was advancing upon the Plains of Dothan.

Dave looked around nervously.

Reb and Jake stood a few feet away. The Southerner had disdained steel armor and was wearing his favorite red shirt, a colorful dot against the duller uniforms of some of the others. He wore his white Stetson shoved back on his head, and now he grinned at Dave and winked. "Looks like the ball's about to start." Looking down the line, he added, "And I reckon we'll be ready for them."

Jake, too, looked down the line of defenders. "Our ranks look pretty thin to me."

"Why, shoot, that don't matter none," Reb said cheerfully. His eyes were electric blue with the thrill of the coming battle. He was at his best in a fight, and now one would have thought he was getting ready to attend a party. He sidled over to Dave and Abbey and Josh and Sarah.

"Looks like you're going to get a fight this time," Josh said. "They're coming."

"Let 'em come. We'll give 'em the best we got at the ranch," Reb said. He winked at Sarah and then looked out over the defenders. "Lots of old friends in this fight today," he said. "There's Volka." He pointed toward a giant who was leaning on a battle club as big as a pine tree. "Old Volk will get his share today, I bet!"

"Aramis and Princess Jere have gone back to

Atlantis," Josh said. "They're having their own battle. The Dark Lord has sent sailors and submariners to attack them."

"They'll do all right," Reb said confidently. "I think I'll just take a little turn around the troops."

Dave watched him walk away, stopping to speak to Eena, who headed a battalion of cave warriors, armed with heavy clubs, spears, and sharp knives. Then, farther along, there was a host of underworld soldiers led by Lord Beren.

"It looks like everybody we've ever met is here," Dave said to Abbey. "There's Captain Daybright and Dawn. And look, there's King Gavin and Queen Merle. Look at those Amazons!"

"They have as much courage as anyone we've ever met in this world," Abbey said. "And see, Reb's found Princess Elaine."

Dave glanced over to where a troop of knights was waiting, mounted on war horses. Gay banners fluttered from the tips of their lances. He saw Reb stop and talk to Princess Elaine, who was herself leading the force from Camelot.

"I guess Reb's glad to see Elaine. He always was soft on her," Dave said. "I hope nothing happens to either one of them."

"Dave," Abbey said and hesitated for a moment, "I'm not really afraid so much for myself, but you be careful."

"I'm always careful."

"You're not really strong enough to be in this battle," she protested. "Why don't you stay back with the archers? You're a good shot."

"No, not this time. I'll be in the front line."

Abbey's lip trembled, and she looked very young

137

and vulnerable. "I've just found you, and now I'm afraid I'm going to lose you."

"You're not going to lose me! We'll be all right," Dave said as cheerfully as he could. He lifted his eyes and saw that now the entire horizon was dark. The sky-line was filled with troops as far back as he could see. "Those are some pretty mean troops coming at us. The Dark Lord has pulled out all the stops, so the reports say."

He felt smaller and smaller as the host that opposed them advanced. When they drew closer, Dave saw that there were not only human adversaries but beasts of all kinds, all looking darkly vicious. A troop of snarling wolves was led on leashes by cruel-looking soldiers. These were not ordinary wolves. They were more than twice the size of normal wolves, he saw, and their eyes were red with rage. In the second rank was a row of war elephants ridden by soldiers wearing gleaming armor. Troops of chunky dwarfs were lined up under the command of a large man on a black horse. Wherever Dave looked, he saw strength and power.

"You'd better get back on that rise with the other archers, Abbey. They're going to hit us soon," Dave said.

Abbey had taken off her helmet, and he reached over suddenly and touched her blonde hair. "I love you, Abbey," he said simply, then impulsively leaned over and kissed her.

"I love you too, Dave," she said, then she walked off to take her place with the line of bowmen.

Abbey found Sarah with the archers. They strung their bows silently, and even as they did so, a trumpet sounded.

A horseman dressed in black armor and a black cloak came galloping out of the enemy host that had stopped two hundred yards away. The hooves of his mighty war horse kicked dust into the air.

He pulled up halfway to Goél's troops. "I am Maulk, champion of the army of the Dark Lord!" The warrior's visor was down, and his voice was muffled. He lifted his spear—its tip gleamed—and said, "The Dark Lord offers you mercy. If you will surrender, you will be well treated. If you will not, then you will all die. What is your answer?"

"You well know our answer."

The voice came from somewhere behind Abbey and Sarah. They looked quickly and saw Goél standing again upon the great flat rock that rose from the surface of the Plains of Dothan. He was wearing his gray cloak as usual, but around his waist was a plain belt that bore the weight of a heavy sword. It was not unsheathed, but Abbey could see the jewels in the handle, glittering in the sunlight.

Goél thrust back his hood. "The hour has struck for the Dark Lord to be answered. Return this answer then. Surrender yourselves to the mercy of Goél before death has his harvest."

The commander laughed hoarsely. "We heed not your words, Goél. Look at yon mighty host—then look at the pitiful line of weaklings that you have! Is this your final answer?" He waited for a moment. When Goél said nothing more, he wheeled and rode back to the enemy position. He then shouted commands, and the orders were echoed by his officers up and down the mighty battle formation.

A mighty shout arose from the Dark Lord's warriors, and Josh watched them surge ahead like a great wave of the sea, rolling forward as though nothing could stop it.

"Here they come!" Reb muttered. "For what we are about to receive may we be truly grateful!"

Beorn, who had positioned himself beside him, looked at the boy and smiled. "Let us stand together, my brother," he said, hefting his battle-ax. "We will see whether this Dark Lord can do as he boasts."

Then suddenly the air was filled with a flight of feathered darts tipped with steel. They struck the first line of the Dark Lord's army, and men and beasts were cut down as if by a mighty scythe. The wolves that had been loosed went down biting and snapping at the keen arrows that dug at their vitals.

"Look at that!" Josh cried. "It's like they ran into a wall!"

"It's a good thing our archers were there," Jake said. He waved briefly back at Abbey and Sarah, hollering, "Good shooting, girls!" Then he turned around toward the advancing enemy line. "They've got plenty of troops to lose." He pulled down his battle helmet and gripped his sword.

On and on came the dark and terrible battalions, rank on rank. The arrows took a mighty toll, but when one beast or one man fell, another was there to step into his place. Soon the first of their number closed the distance between the forces.

Reb leaped forward eagerly. Josh, Dave, and Beorn were close beside him. A swarthy giant of a soldier, his eyes glittering, cried out and swung his sword. Reb simply ducked under it and with almost a graceful movement reached out and struck with his own blade.

Both sides hacked and slashed, and the cries of the wounded and the dying soon filled the air.

Then the mighty centaurs led by Moonwise suddenly appeared and struck the enemy's flank, sending them reeling. Many fled in terror as the arrows of the centaurs wrought death and destruction.

The Aluks hit the soldiers of the Dark Lord on their other flank, many of them casting harpoons. These deadly weapons struck among the battle elephants, causing them to rear and panic. They trampled many of the enemy in their frantic efforts to flee.

Still, there was no stopping the mighty wave of warriors and beasts. Slowly Goél's ranks were forced to give way. And as the Sleepers moved back, they saw they were leaving the bodies of many brave friends who had paid with their blood for their resistance.

Time and time again, the warriors of Goél stopped and dug in their heels and fought for their lives. But then came the strongest attack of all! The Dark Lord brought his own archers into play along with machines that hurled huge stones. The stones and the arrows took their toll, and the Sleepers saw more dear friends fall lifeless to the earth.

As they withdrew, Jake yelled a warning to Josh— two soldiers were about to attack him from behind! Josh whirled just in time to see Jake throw himself at the warriors. Jake managed to deflect the blade of one. But while his attention was taken, the other leaped at him, swinging a huge sword.

Josh knew that his friend was in danger of being felled. He took a step to help, but just then their section of the line came under violent attack. Josh fought like a madman, as did the others, to drive off the assault. As soon as he could, he ran back to where he'd left Jake.

Jake was on the ground, trying to sit up.

"Jake . . ." Josh dropped his sword and knelt beside him. "I'll get you back with the wounded."

"No," Jake whispered, "they've—done it for me this time, Josh."

"Don't say that!"

Jake lay back and reached out a hand, and Josh took it. "You've been the best," he whispered. His eyelids fluttered, but he managed a smile. "Think about me sometimes . . ." Then his eyes closed.

Josh heard Dave and Reb speaking to him, but he could not tell what they were saying. At last he stood and brushed his tears away. "Jake's gone."

The three young men stood silent, filled with grief, and finally they carried Jake's body back behind the lines where he was borne away.

"He was a good soldier," Reb said softly. His eyes were gentle, then thoughtful. "I'll miss him. We all will."

Then Dave cried, "The Dark Lord's troops—here they come again!"

The soldiers of the Dark Lord seemed to be inexhaustible. No matter how many were slain, there were always more!

Slowly the thin line of defenders was forced to yield again. By late afternoon, their backs were against the wall of the mountain that rose on the eastern side of the plain. Here defense was somewhat easier because they had the high ground and the attackers had to dodge around gullies, which made them easier prey for the archers.

On and on the battle raged until the sun was ready to go down. It dipped at last behind the ridge of mountains, and the air grew cooler.

In the quiet that followed, Dave wiped his brow with a trembling hand. He gasped, "I guess . . . that's all for today."

"They'll be back in the morning," Reb said grimly. "We better get what rest we can."

And then Goél stood before them. He looked at them with compassion in his eyes.

"You have done well. Valiant warriors all," he said quietly.

Josh shook his head. "Jake is dead," he said simply.

"Yes, I know."

"That's hard, sire," Dave said, almost in a whisper. "First Wash and now Jake. Two out of the seven of us gone."

Goél rested his gray eyes on Dave and said, "Not two. Three, my son."

Dave stopped breathing. He whispered, "Not . . . Abbey?"

"Yes, she died like a warrior. Bravely, fighting for me and for the House of Goél."

Dave looked faint, almost unable to stand.

Goél made no attempt to say more. He simply stood with them, his face weary with strain. When he did speak again, he said only, "Your two companions have paid the ultimate price. Are you still willing to fight for Goél?"

Dave nodded, despite the visible agony of grief that was in him. Reb and Josh did the same.

Goél's eyes suddenly seemed to burn, and he cried, "I knew I could count on your love and loyalty. The struggle will not be for long." Then he turned away and vanished into the growing darkness. Josh could hear him going down the line, encouraging others of his troops.

The three boys sat down and were soon joined by Sarah and Beorn. No one could speak for grief and did not try to for some time. Dave finally rose to his feet and walked off into the darkness.

"He was in love with Abbey," Sarah said, "and she with him."

"Yes," Josh said awkwardly. He looked over at Sarah. "It may be me tomorrow. Or you—I couldn't stand that, Sarah!"

"We will stand whatever we have to," Sarah said, her head thrown back. She dashed away her tears. "For as long as we live, what Wash, and Jake, and Abbey have died for will live. Their lives aren't lost."

Josh nodded slowly, and then they too walked away, hand in hand.

Reb and Beorn watched them go.

Beorn said, "I had a love like that once."

It might have sounded ridiculous, an ugly, stumpy dwarf speaking of love, but somehow it did not. Reb knew what the dwarf meant. He moved over to sit beside Beorn and said, "Tomorrow I think we will all die."

"All must someday die," Beorn said calmly, "and we will join our friends in death. We will have died with honor and dignity, and nothing else is important at a time like this when the sky is falling!"

14

The Terror

The Dark Lord himself advanced to watch the battle. For three days he had sent wave after wave of troops against the thin line of defenders who had their backs against the mountains of Dothan. Time and again he had seen the devoted followers of Goél withstand the charges of his powerful battalions. He had also attempted, through the use of his spiritual powers, to overcome the minds and bring fear into the hearts of his enemies. This effort had failed, however, for Deormi and her wise men were able to withstand this sort of attack.

He had lost three commanders in action, and now the newly appointed commander, a short, powerful, dwarflike creature named Lothag, stood before him. Lothag was bloodied, and he trembled from fatigue. He had just come back to the command position of the Dark Lord, who awaited his report.

"My liege lord," Lothag said wearily, "we have done all that can be done."

"You have *failed!*" the Dark Lord spat. He reached forth as if he would slay his commander with his own hand, but then changed his mind. "You're no better than the rest, but the next might be worse. Come," he said, "and bring two battalions of our best troops."

Lothag blinked with surprise. "And where shall I lead them?"

"Back to the Dread Tower."

Lothag did not pretend to understand but went to

145

quickly assemble his weary troops. In truth, they had suffered terribly, and there was no time for burial. When he had gathered his forces together, they mounted swift horses and began the return journey. The Dark Lord rode on ahead, leaving a dire warning for them to hurry.

When they reached the Dread Tower, the gate opened, and the weary horses, barely able to stand, staggered through it. The soldiers, in little better shape than their horses, fell from their mounts and reeled to the well to slake their thirst. Lothag considered calling them, lashing out at them, telling them to act like soldiers, but he muttered, "They've done all men can do."

He turned and straightened his shoulders. He had not chosen to be the commander of the Dark Lord's host, but it had fallen to his lot. Now he walked stiffly into the tower and went directly past all the guards to the Dark Lord's throne room. He knocked and heard a gruff, "Come in."

"We are here, sire."

"You took long enough about it, but no matter. We'll not speak of that now." The Dark Lord was striding back and forth. His cowl was about his head, and his red eyes glittered as he paced the floor. "I would not have thought that ragtag army could have withstood all of our forces."

"They are men and beasts determined to sell their lives dearly—and so they have," Lothag muttered.

"Well, they will not last long."

"We cannot take those rocks, sire. I must tell you that."

"Perhaps not, but there is another way. Come with me." The Dark Lord spoke to a lieutenant at the door. "Have every soldier, every man available, mounted on a fresh horse. Empty the tower. We will all go back to fight in this battle."

The lieutenant blinked. "Yes, my lord."

"And we will have . . . *help* . . . on this foray."

Lothag glanced at the Dark Lord. He had never before seen him hesitate, but there was something in his manner now that was different. "What is this help, if I may ask, sire?"

"Come, and you shall see."

The Dark Lord led Lothag down a series of stone steps. Deeper and deeper into the bowels of the earth they descended. The darkness was broken by torches fastened in iron holders driven into the wall. The light flickered over the cruel features of the Dark Lord.

Lothag—stout soldier though he was—had to force himself to follow. He had heard stories of the depths of the Dread Tower and of what lay here, but he had never believed them. He'd merely scoffed, "Old wives' tales! There's nothing there but maybe a wine cellar." But now . . .

Finally they reached the lowest level, an arching room, its ceiling held up by gigantic braces of huge stone.

"This way," the Dark Lord said. He took a large key from his pocket and unlocked a brass door that glowed dully in the guttering torchlight. "Come, and do not let your courage fail."

"My courage has never failed, sire!"

"But you have never seen this," the Dark Lord said. He himself drew his back straighter, and his features, even under the shadow of the cowl, looked tense.

Lothag could not imagine what lay beyond that door.

"Come," the Dark Lord said again, detaching a wall torch. He pulled the door open to reveal a tunnel.

The Dark Lord led the way, holding the torch before him. They made several turns before coming to the most shocking thing of all. Suddenly Lothag found himself in a gigantic cavern. Stalactites glistened like huge icicles. Millions of bats left the ceiling with a roar like thunder as their leathery wings beat the air.

"Here it is," the Dark Lord said, ignoring the sound. He waved his torch, and Lothag bent forward. He could not see in the murkiness. "What is it, sire?"

"The door to the pit!"

And then Lothag saw that, indeed, at the center of the cavern floor was what appeared to be another door of heavy brass. It was fully fifty feet across and was secured to the solid stone with huge steel bolts. Some apparatus was attached to the ceiling above it, with cables descending and fastening themselves to a massive ring.

Lothag swallowed hard. "The door . . . to the pit, my lord?"

The Dark Lord seemed not to have heard him. He was muttering, "I thought never to open this—but now I have no choice." He moved to the cave wall where a single lever extended. "Come here," he said. "You see where the tunnel continues?"

Lothag looked to where a large blackness gaped.

"Yes, I see it."

"That tunnel will take us to the surface. But now, take heed. When I open the door to the pit you will meet something you have never seen before." The Dark Lord licked his lips nervously. "You may call it The Terror, if you please."

Something in the words *The Terror* struck that very emotion in Lothag. Something was not human about this, something he could not identify. His hands began to tremble. "Sire, what—what is it?"

"The Terror comes from the bowels of the earth. It has been bound in this pit for longer than men's minds go back. Even before Oldworld was destroyed, The Terror was here, and now we must loose it."

"But, sire, what *is* it?"

"It is a foul spirit. No—more than that. It is a foul *presence*. I cannot say whether it is flesh. I was able to control it once, but it has had centuries to nurse its resentment. When I pull this lever, you and I both may be annihilated."

"Then do not pull it, sire!"

"I will! I must! I will defeat Goél. He cannot stand against The Terror. I will control it. Yes, I will control it."

The Dark Lord leaned on the lever. There was a creaking, and some obscure machinery began to grind.

Lothag watched in horror as the cables tightened. He wished they would break. Whatever was under that massive gate, he did not want to see.

But the cables did not break. A sudden snapping sound echoed in Lothag's ears, and then the brass plate lifted slowly. It cleared the opening, swung to one side, and dropped with a clanking onto the stone floor.

For some few moments there was no further sound, nothing at all, and Lothag hoped fervently that whatever was in that hole had died! But then there came a distant rumbling, and it sent horror through him. He would have run, but his legs seemed to have failed him, they trembled so violently.

And then he saw it!

Up out of the darkness rose something even blacker than that from which it arose. It was impossible to tell the shape. It was like a swirling, angry cloud, and inside it was flashing lightning. It was more monstrous than anything had ever been.

The Dark Lord approached it. "I command you, come with me. You must fight my battles!"

A hissing sound emerged from the center of the darkness that marked the creature—whatever it was—and the lightning flashes grew brighter. The thing moved forward.

The Dark Lord threw up a hand and began to speak words that Lothag could not understand. The commander fell to his knees, for fear drained him of his manhood. He saw the shadow touch the very robe of the Dark Lord—and then stop.

The Dark Lord gasped, but then he said, "Now, follow me, commander!"

Lothag scrambled to his feet. He could not run quickly enough to get to the tunnel toward which the Dark Lord moved. Anything to get away from The Terror!

They reached the tunnel opening and entered darkness that was broken only by their single torch. Behind them, a high-pitched keening sounded, growing steadily louder as they hurried upward toward the surface. Then they emerged, and Lothag saw that they were outside the walls of the Dread Tower.

The Dark Lord lifted his voice to the sentry. "Bring out the troops. We move to the Plains of Dothan."

"What will happen?" Lothag gasped, his mouth dry with fear.

"You will see. Goél's forces may stand against human assault, but they will never stand against this." He waved his hand at the blob of darkness that had issued from the tunnel behind them.

The Terror, Lothag saw, had a changing form continually, and little wisps of fire showed themselves from within the depths of the awful, beastlike creature.

"Now, we will see if Goél will stand! He will not! They will all die!" the Dark Lord cried. He mounted the battle horse a soldier brought forward. "Come, Lothag. Now, we will see how goes the battle."

"What's going on?" Josh asked wearily. Battling had drained him dry, and grief for his lost companions was a constant pain. Strangely, the Dark Lord's forces had abruptly withdrawn two days earlier, but now Josh saw something moving on the horizon. "Get the men up," he said to Beorn. "They're coming back."

The warriors pulled themselves to their feet, tested their weapons, and reformed their line. They stood silently waiting, watching the battle lines of the Dark Lord form.

But then Josh saw something strange and new.

"The lines are parting," Reb said. "What's that coming through the middle?" He shaded his eyes. "I don't know what *that* is, but it's not good."

"Some monkey business of the Dark Lord," Dave muttered. "Well, we'll just have to stand against it."

And then a tall figure—it was the Dark Lord himself—rode forth, trailed by a man in the uniform of a commander. He rode to within calling distance and shouted, "Goél, show yourself!"

"I am here." The answer came at once in ringing tones. "What would you have of me?"

The Dark Lord laughed wildly. "I would have your life and the lives of those who have served you. You have had your chance to surrender. Now, once more I will offer your followers my mercy."

Goél stepped into view, still wearing his gray garb and the sword at his side. "I well know *your* mercy.

You have shown it in your enslavement of my people. What would you have with me?" he asked again.

The Dark Lord shook his head. "This ends your puny reign! The House of Goél falls this day. Its foundations are shaken." He looked back, made a forward motion with his hand, and screamed a command.

Josh blinked at what happened next. "What's *that?*" he said.

Sarah was beside him. "I don't know. It looks like a cloud, a black cloud."

"Look at Goél!" Dave cried at the top of his lungs, and the Sleepers all turned toward their leader.

Goél was advancing toward the black cloud, and as he advanced he drew his sword. It glittered in the sunlight. With his free hand he stripped off the gray outer robe and threw it aside.

"I've never seen him like *that!*" Sarah whispered.

Underneath his robe Goél wore a white garment— no, it was more than white. It would have put white to shame. It glowed like light itself. His head held high, he raised the sword, saying, "You have brought The Terror? We shall see then who will rule Nuworld!"

A cry went up from both armies as the dark shadow of The Terror rolled forward. There was a crackling in the air, and inside the darkness of the beast were flashings of fire. One flash lashed out toward the figure of Goél. He met it with a slash of his gleaming sword. A deep roar burst from The Terror. Then the thing threw itself forward, and the two armies could do nothing but watch as the adversaries met.

Goél's sword flashed quicker than light as The Terror's fiery rays tried to envelop him. He took more than one blow, but he was singing as he wielded the sword, and it was a song of victory.

Josh could hear the words. He didn't know if the

enemy could understand the song; Goél's followers did. It told of the courage of those who had followed him. It spoke of the love of comradeship, the love of one soldier for another—and be they men or women, that love would never die. There was comfort for Goél's people in the song. But Josh could not understand how their leader could sing so victoriously when it appeared he would be overwhelmed by a monster such as this one.

The roar of The Terror split the air. It threw itself forward time and again, only to be thrust back by the flashing, wheeling sword of Goél. The creature's voice was hoarse and shrill at the same time. It crackled with fury. It was as if all the thunderstorms in the world had bound themselves into this one awful, dark cloud and now were determined to annihilate the tall, glowing figure that stood against it so valiantly!

Josh did not know how long the battle raged, but suddenly he realized that the tide had turned. Goél took a step forward and then another. And another. The fiery tentacles lashed out, but he laughed aloud and said, "Taste now the wrath of Goél!" He ran toward The Terror then and seemed to throw himself into the very depths of the monster's darkness!

Josh's heart almost stopped when that happened, but then he cried, "Look—look at it, Sarah!"

Sarah was indeed looking, staring.

The Terror seemed to fly apart. The flashing sword of Goél reached its vitals. Its darkness grew gray . . . broke into tiny fragments . . . and then it was gone!

A sudden, mighty cry of victory went up all along the line of Goél's army.

Goél turned to his followers. "Come, my children," he cried. "The day is ours!"

That was all the army needed! Goél led the way.

The Sleepers rushed forward, Reb Jackson in the lead, waving his sword and giving the Confederate Rebel cry.

The army of the Dark Lord turned on its heels. They fled in terror, led in their retreat by the Dark Lord himself, who turned his horse's head back toward the tower.

"Come!" he screamed. "They cannot get at us inside the tower. Fight your way back. Hold an honorable retreat!"

Josh laughed at this and slapped Reb on the back, who in turn slapped Beorn's back, and then Dave joined them, and then Sarah.

"Let's see if he can stop this bunch," Reb yelled.

And thus the final battle began, and Josh knew that there would be no end until the Dark Lord bowed his knee to Goél.

15

Good-bye to Old Friends

The Dread Tower stood like a lean, black forefinger pointing to the sky. The Dark Lord and his followers had frantically retreated to their citadel, and now he marched around the parapet, muttering as he watched Goél's host gathering outside, preparing for attack. Turning to his commander, he snapped, "We should charge them!"

"No, my lord!" Lothag exclaimed. He had seen the fiery light in the eyes of the attackers and knew that his own men were exhausted by the retreat. Most had dropped their weapons and now were manning the walls with whatever they could find. Some had only clubs. "We will be fortunate if we can stand off their attack."

The Dark Lord snarled, "You always were a coward, Lothag!"

Lothag straightened up but did not answer. He had lost hope but dared not say so. If the Dark Lord had been any other, he might have suggested surrender, but one look at the wrath on his leader's face told him that such a recommendation was useless.

"We will do what men can do, sire," he said stiffly. His thought was, *If The Terror could not overcome Goél's forces, how can our poor remnants hope to do so?* But aloud he said, "I will make the rounds and try to shore up our defense."

Outside the Dread Tower, Goél stood with his captains grouped around him. The battle had been fierce, but still his raiment seemed to glow, and there was a noble light on his face that encouraged all of his weary commanders—among them what remained of the Seven Sleepers.

Goél's eyes went from face to face. He said, "Never have men fought so bravely, but our task is not done." He pointed firmly. "We *will* take that tower." Then he whirled back to them and seemed to examine the soul of each one. "Are you willing to try?" He knew they were exhausted, that each had lost dear friends, and that their hearts were sore.

It was Josh Adams who said, as he straightened his shoulders, "We will try, my lord."

"That's my brave young commander!" Goél smiled. He shook Josh's hand, then went around the circle and shook every hand. "This day will be recorded and sung as the greatest victory of the House of Goél," he said. "Now, go to your places, and when you hear the sound of the trumpet, do not look back to see who is following."

Wearily, Josh and the other Sleepers returned to their positions. The attacking line was thin. And he well knew that, as soon as they came within range of the archers on the parapets, others would fall. Nevertheless Josh smiled and slapped the back of every member of his small command, saying, "Now we will show them what we can do."

"I reckon we will, Josh. I trust you to tote the key to the smokehouse." It was the highest compliment Reb could pay, and he smiled widely as he said it.

Dave had not smiled since hearing of the death of Abbey, but now he did. "I don't mind dying now," he said, "if that's the way it goes." He looked toward the Dread Tower. "I want the House of Goél to rule over the earth. That's all that really counts."

"I feel the same way, Dave," Sarah said. Then she moved a little closer to Josh so that her arm touched his. They did not speak, but, somehow, as they looked at each other, volumes were spoken.

Suddenly the blare of a trumpet smote the morning air, and a cry went up from thousands of throats. "The Tower! Down with the Tower! Down with the Dark Lord!" And Josh led his people forward.

Goél's troops attacked the walls, and some fell from the arrows that flew from overhead. On pressed the others toward the gate. They were met with flashing swords, and once again the air was filled with the shouts of rage and the cries of the wounded and the dying.

Josh fought until he thought his sword arm would fall off from weariness. More than once he felt the swords of his enemies, but he paid no heed. He was crying, "On for Goél! On for Wash! Remember Abbey! Remember our loyal Jake!"

His cries were taken up, and the portal was taken. The survivors of Goél's forces swarmed through.

He saw Goél stride to the center of the courtyard and engage the Dark Lord in a fierce duel. It was darkness against light, good against evil, love against hate. The two fought furiously, the shining raiment of Goél contrasting vividly with the ebony robes of the Dark Lord.

"Whatever you say about the Dark Lord, he's strong," Reb said with reluctant admiration, as their enemy fought desperately against Goél's flashing sword.

But it was useless. Suddenly Goél struck his enemy's sword and sent it wheeling through the air. Instantly Goél put his blade to the throat of his adversary.

Silence fell, and then the soldiers of the Dark Lord

began throwing down their weapons and begging for mercy.

As the victory cry went up, Josh felt blood seeping inside his armor and knew that he had been wounded worse than he'd thought. But he whispered hoarsely, "We've won."

He looked around and saw Sarah lying still amid a ring of the fallen enemy. He staggered to her, lifted her head. She was smiling, and her eyes were closed as if she were asleep, but he saw that she was not asleep. And then Josh felt a touch. He looked up to see Goél standing over him.

"Come, my brave warrior, you must see this."

"But Sarah—"

"Come with me first."

Josh staggered to his feet. He could barely stand, but Goél's strong hand helped him.

"You saw the beginning," Goél said gently, "and now you must see the end, my brave Joshua."

Josh would have fallen, except that Goél swept the boy up in his arms. "Come into the tower," he cried to his followers. "Bring the Dark Lord."

Josh could not see what was happening. His head felt light. He could sense, though, that they were going down many steps and through a tunnel. At last he was set on his feet.

"Stand here, my boy," Goél said. "It will soon be over."

Josh leaned against the stone wall, then slumped to the ground, holding his bloody side. And then he saw a large opening in the floor.

The Dark Lord stood in front of it. His face was twisted with fear, and he began to cry for mercy.

The voice of Goél cut like a knife. "You have shown no mercy. Now you will know none."

Goél seized the Dark Lord in his mighty grasp. Despite Josh's dimming sight, he saw the brief final struggle between the two. Then the Dark Lord was cast into the pit and some machinery whirred. A massive lid swung through the air and clamped down.

"Lock it! Lock it forever!" Goél cried, and Josh saw soldiers tightening the mighty door into place with huge bolts.

Then Josh felt himself losing consciousness. Hands touched him—he sensed they were Goél's hands—and he opened his eyes with great effort. He tried to speak but could not.

He heard the voice of Goél say, "My faithful Joshua. Great is your courage!"

And then Josh Adams heard no more. Darkness swept over him, and his last thought was, *I wish I could've said good-bye to Sarah.*

16

The Quest of
the Seven Sleepers

Somewhere a bird was singing.

Josh had never heard this particular bird before, but he knew its song was the sweetest sound that he had ever heard come from a bird's throat. For a long time he lay quietly, his eyes closed, pleasure flowing through him as the song came through the air, entered his ears, and went down deep into his heart. It was a song of love, of loyalty, and of goodness. Josh felt that he could have listened to it forever.

When the song faded away, Josh was aware of warm sunshine on his face. It was as if he had been asleep after a tiring day and was now waking up refreshed and touched in every inch of his body by a feeling of well-being and ease.

He opened his eyes just a fraction and saw the green leaves of the tree shading him from the sun overhead. The tree itself seemed to give off a pleasant scent. Looking again, he saw the branches were filled with fruit, but it was a fruit he did not recognize, and he thought, *If that fruit tastes as good as it smells, it'll be the best I ever ate.*

He became aware then of the soft grass that lay underneath him. He opened his eyes wider, then sat up suddenly and looked around. He found himself surrounded by grass so green that it almost hurt his eyes. It reminded him of pictures he had once seen of Ireland, where the greenery seemed beyond belief. The earth itself was soft, and he felt its warmth.

Rising to his feet, Josh was conscious of a tremendous sense of health and strength. He wanted to run and shout. As his eyes swept the trees and the grass, the blue sky and the white clouds that floated across it like huge puffs of cotton, he felt as he never had before in his life.

He noticed he was wearing a garment of light blue silk, and he somehow remembered that he had been terribly wounded in the side. Pulling up his shirt, he looked but saw no sign of a scar. He was puzzled.

He began to walk and saw other trees bearing different fruits. He picked one, a firm red globe, not an apple but perfectly round. When he tasted it, the juice flowed down his throat, cool and sweet and yet tangy. It was the best juice he had ever tasted. Farther along was a bush filled with bright purple berries, sweeter than ripe blackberries. They had their own special taste that was a delight to the tongue and a fragrance that was a delight to smell.

As he walked, Josh sensed that things had changed. He suddenly remembered a battle, one that seemed to have happened long ago. And then memory came back to him more sharply. The faces of friends floated up before him. Sarah and Abbey. He saw them as clearly as if they stood before him in their girlish beauty. He thought of other friends—Wash and Jake, Dave and Reb. He could not tell if he had been thinking of them for a long time or only briefly. Indeed, he had no idea if he had been wandering in this beautiful forest for only a few moments or for weeks, or months, or even years. Something seemed to have happened to time.

"There is my Joshua!"

Josh stopped and looked up, then joy filled him.

162

"Goél!" he cried and ran to meet him. He ran easily over the grass, almost floating. There was no effort at all to the moving. He dropped to his knees before Goél and felt hands on his head. Then he felt himself being lifted up, and Goél's gray eyes were upon him.

"Come," Goél said, "I have much to say to you." He was wearing a white robe that glowed like sunshine, and he looked different somehow.

They began to walk together, and as Goél talked, Josh was moved to both joy and grief. Strangely mingled, memories came back of times he had walked with Goél before. Once Josh began to speak of an occasion when he had failed Goél, and shame touched him briefly, like a feather brushing over his soul.

"Those times are part of you and of me," Goél said simply, "but you have been faithful, and now we will remember the good."

Josh had another thought, and though he did not speak it aloud, he saw Goél smile.

"Do you have questions, my son?"

"Where *is* this place?"

"It is the place you have always longed for."

"It's not like Nuworld. It looks different. Everything is brighter."

"It is the *real* world, Joshua. Oldworld and Nuworld have passed away. They had their time, but now we are here."

The two walked for a long time—or for a short time. Whatever it was, it was a period when Josh seemed to soak in the very presence of Goél.

"Look ahead," Goél said. "There are some you know."

Josh looked, and suddenly joy overflowed. "Sarah!" he cried. He ran forward, and there she was—and yet it was not the Sarah he remembered!

163

The last time he had seen her, he recalled vaguely, she had been lying on the earth, bloodstained and cold. Now her eyes were bright, her cheeks glowed with health, and her lips were red as she smiled at him.

She reached out and took his hands. "Josh!" she said. "We meet again."

"Sarah, are you all right?"

She laughed merrily. "Why would I not be all right?"

"I don't know," Josh said. "I'm a little confused."

Then suddenly they all were there, Jake and Wash and Abbey and Dave and Reb. The air was filled with the sound of their delighted cries, and Wash—who now seemed somehow bigger than he had been—said, "I told you I'd see you again, and here I am."

"Yes, you did, Wash." Josh hugged the boy impulsively and then stepped back. "All of you, you look . . . you look like you're . . . well, like you're filled with light."

Light did seem to be emanating from all of them, and Josh was suddenly aware that probably he looked different in their sight.

Goél was watching with a smile.

Sarah turned to him and said, "I feel at home here, Goél."

"Yes, it's your real home. The one you always longed for, Sarah."

Reb was stamping the ground happily. "This is my real country."

"Come, children, it is time for our first meal together."

No one would ever forget that meal—but then did they ever forget *anything* from that moment on?

They ate food that seemed to melt in their mouths, they drank wine that cheered but did not intoxicate, they laughed, and slowly the memories flooded back. It was strange that they could remember the hard times without grief. They could remember sorrows that had been keen but were now no longer painful. They talked and talked and talked.

Goél was sitting at the head of the table, and there was a cup in front of him. He smiled and said, "I drink to the health of the Seven Sleepers." He drank and passed the silver cup to Josh, who was sitting at his right hand. Josh drank, and the cup went around the table. Finally, it came full circle to Reb, who sat at Goél's left, and Josh thought they all looked full and satisfied and happy.

"Now it is time to begin," Goél said.

Faraway cliffs rose high into the air, higher than any cliffs the Sleepers had ever seen. They looked at a mountain that kept going up and up and up until it pierced the sky.

"Where are we going, Goél?" Josh asked.

"It is time for you to begin your quest."

"Our *quest?* But—I thought that was over!"

Goél laughed, and it was a happy laugh. His white teeth flashed. "That was training. Now our real work begins. Are you ready for it, my children?"

Josh Adams remembered the first time he had seen Goél. He had asked Josh that same question. He looked at Sarah and saw that she was thinking of the same thing. Somehow, amazingly, he was in her mind and she in his. They were both thinking of the times of danger and toil and learning, and they were also thinking, *It's not over.*

Sarah thought, *It will never be over, will it?*

Josh, without opening his lips, responded, *No, it never will.*

As they moved toward the mountain, they were

joined by a multitude of old friends and Nuworld creatures.

Josh saw his father and mother, and he greeted them with love. He saw Moonwise the centaur, except that now he seemed to be a golden horse with silver hair. He began to recognize still others and somehow knew that all Goél's people were here, hurrying with him toward the great mountain.

"Onward!" Goél cried. "Are you ready, my children?"

Josh Adams answered for them all. "Yes! This is better than anything, isn't it?"

Sarah turned to look into his eyes, and she smiled. "Yes, it is. Now, Josh, we can really begin to live!"

The procession flowed joyously up the mountain as Goél led them into a shining new world.

The Seven Sleepers had begun their final and everlasting quest!

Get swept away in the many Gilbert Morris Adventures available from Moody Press:

"Too Smart" Jones

4025-8 Pool Party Thief
4026-6 Buried Jewels
4027-4 Disappearing Dogs
4028-2 Dangerous Woman
4029-0 Stranger in the Cave
4030-4 Cat's Secret
4031-2 Stolen Bicycle
4032-0 Wilderness Mystery
4033-9 Spooky Mansion
4034-7 Mysterious Artist

Come along for the adventures and mysteries Juliet "Too Smart" Jones always manages to find. She and her other homeschool friends solve these great adventures and learn biblical truths along the way. Ages 9-14

Seven Sleepers - The Lost Chronicles

3667-6 The Spell of the Crystal Chair
3668-4 The Savage Game of Lord Zarak
3669-2 The Strange Creatures of Dr. Korbo
3670-6 City of the Cyborgs
3671-4 The Temptations of Pleasure Island
3672-2 Victims of Nimbo
3673-0 The Terrible Beast of Zor

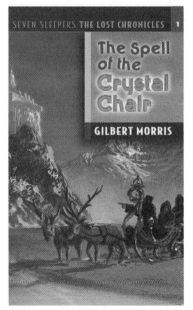

More exciting adventures from the Seven Sleepers. As these exciting young people attempt to faithfully follow Goél, they learn important moral and spiritual lessons. Come along with them as they encounter danger, intrigue, and mystery. Ages 10-14

MOODY
The Name You Can Trust
1-800-678-8812 www.MoodyPress.org

Dixie Morris Animal Adventures

3363-4 Dixie and Jumbo
3364-2 Dixie and Stripes
3365-0 Dixie and Dolly
3366-9 Dixie and Sandy
3367-7 Dixie and Ivan
3368-5 Dixie and Bandit
3369-3 Dixie and Champ
3370-7 Dixie and Perry
3371-5 Dixie and Blizzard
3382-3 Dixie and Flash

Follow the exciting adventures of this animal lover as she learns more of God and His character through her many adventures underneath the Big Top.
Ages 9-14

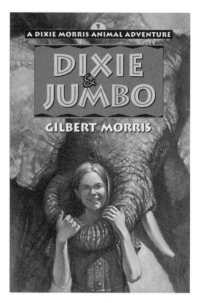

The Daystar Voyages

4102-X Secret of the Planet Makon
4106-8 Wizards of the Galaxy
4107-6 Escape From the Red Comet
4108-4 Dark Spell Over Morlandria
4109-2 Revenge of the Space Pirates
4110-6 Invasion of the Killer Locusts
4111-4 Dangers of the Rainbow Nebula
4112-2 The Frozen Space Pilot
4113-0 White Dragon of Sharnu
4114-9 Attack of the Denebian Starship

Join the crew of the Daystar as they traverse the wide expanse of space. Adventure and danger abound, but they learn time and again that God is truly the Master of the Universe.
Ages 10-14

MOODY
The Name You Can Trust
1-800-678-8812 www.MoodyPress.org